UNBELIEVABLE

Introducing *A Need to Know* About UFOs, ETs, Technology, Economics, and Politics

---

This book is provided by the author for your reading enjoyment.

T. C. K.

If you choose to read it, please submit a customer review on Amazon.com

Go to their website and search *UNBELIEVABLE – A Need to Know*. Then

scroll down to "Customer Reviews" click on "Write a customer review".

Thank you.

UNBELIEVABLE

Introducing *A Need to Know* About UFOs, ETs, Technology, Economics, and Politics

Tim C. King

UNBELIEVABLE
Introducing A Need to Know About
UFOs, ETs, Technology, Economics, and Politics

ISBN: 979-8-3231-1260-9

DEDICATION

This is built entirely upon the dedicated individuals seeking to reveal the truth. These are the unsung heroes. Many have faced ridicule, humiliation, and threats; with some having been attacked or even murdered.

CONTENTS

PREFACE

Welcome to the topic of Extraterrestrials (ETs) and Unidentified Flying Objects (UFOs). There's so much to cover on this topic. There are thousands of books, articles, YouTube videos, and other online information sources. You'd think everything has been covered. But, as a result of my studies, I've made some surprising discoveries. This is aimed at answering both the common questions that many people have, along with ones that have remained unanswered until now.

The topic of ETs and UFOs covers a number of broad areas, including alien civilizations, science, spirituality, governments, politics, economics, technologies, and history, to name a few. Most of these quickly rise to the surface in any investigation into this subject. As a result, these will be addressed as well. The reader will be skeptical of some of the answers provided, but they will lend credibility to the overall phenomenon and hopefully lead to further interest and study.

I'm not trying to change minds here, but provide answers to both obvious and hidden questions. And, in doing so, it will expand your perspective and prompt further thought. This is for your information; expanding your knowledge, perspective, and awareness.

One thing is certain, the information will provide new insights that will be most unexpected.

PART I OVERVIEW

UNBELIEVABLE

CHAPTER 1 INTRODUCTION

"Truth is stranger than fiction, but it is because Fiction is obliged to stick to possibilities; Truth isn't."

Mark Twain

This is the guiding theme for this book. As you'll soon discover, this famous quote aptly describes this topic as it's presented here. If you're interested in the underlying truth about Unidentified Flying Objects (UFOs) and Extraterrestrials (ETs), this book is for you. And it's aimed at readers of all levels. Whether you have a casual or general interest, or even for the most informed students and investigators of the UFO/ET phenomenon; you'll find startling answers to both common and hidden questions. It won't disappoint.

Are UFOs and ETs real? Why are they such a secret? Why don't ETs reveal themselves? What do they want? Are they a threat? And, finally, what about Disclosure?

You'll find all of these and more answered here. And, surprisingly, many will become fairly obvious as you learn more. Other questions, though, are rarely asked and – to my knowledge – have remained unanswered until now. These will be among the most unbelievable. And, despite their making complete sense, they'll still trigger disbelief at best and quite likely abject denial. This reaction is simply unavoidable and needs to be recognized upfront. It's the real challenge every reader will face. And, it is the reason for the reference to Mark Twain's quote. This will present the unbelievable.

Thus, while this isn't fiction, readers might want to view it as such to overcome the obstacle of total denial of the truth. But, in the end, and regardless of your assessment of the validity of any of the contents, you'll have an entirely new perspective on the topic of UFOs/ETs, as well as everything else relating to it. And, this is the aim.

Overview

Another difference with this book is it's atypical of most of this genre. The focus is not on the details. Most UFO/ET books cite specific encounters, observed phenomena, or experiences. This is primarily for two reasons. First, it appeals to most reader's interests. And second, it's to convey the reality of the existence of UFOs and ETs. While I will also cite specific examples, this is done to 1) further illustrate the validity of the evidence and 2) build the case leading to logical conclusions. It's a necessary part of the process.

This book has a deeper goal. It's not to convince the reader of their reality. This book is about suggesting what is really going on. It's what you don't see. This becomes clearly evident once you take a step back after extensive study. It's about the secrecy, underlying history, politics, and economics. Along with how ETs have been involved behind the scenes in collaborative and subversive roles for over a century.

Can't See the Forest for the Trees
If you get so engrossed in the details, you don't realize what is really behind it all. If you follow the news, you know the U.S. Government has recently acknowledged the existence of UFOs. But ETs and all the related questions still remain. By examining the underlying history, economics, and politics involved; it leads to far more pertinent questions. And these, are still out of sight. They are being avoided by a continuing superficial focus on evidence and technology. As you'll learn, this is no accident. Thus, the focus here is on the trees. It's to gain an overview and understanding of what's really involved with the UFO and ET phenomenon. And it's certainly not what most people think. This is the objective.

The Real Challenge
As a result, I guarantee you will react to the answers provided – ranging from complete denial to abject skepticism. With the information being presented, this is unavoidable and it's to be expected. For, belief in what's being presented is not the goal. It's totally unreasonable. And, it's not simply a matter of the credibility of the evidence, but more so the emotional reaction everyone will face. Some of the facts undermine what we've not only been taught, what everyone believes, and what we've all taken for granted. This is an assault on our senses.

The challenge here is to continue reading, despite your doubts or denial.

INTRODUCTION

Regardless of everything presented being evidence-based, it's simply too fantastic. It's too contrary to what everyone thinks is truth. We've all been led down the garden path. The truth has been concealed, and, as you'll learn, for good reason. Thus, it's completely unrealistic to expect anyone to believe the incredible reality of what's presented in this book. It turns out Mr. Twain had a remarkable insight.

Goals
The goal isn't for you to necessarily believe what is being presented. It's to gain an appreciation of 1) the depth and scope of the topic, 2) the extensive and consistent evidence, 3) an entirely new perspective on the potential for a completely new reality, 4) its hidden importance, 5) an expanded awareness, 6) your consideration and thought, and finally, 7) answers to both known and previously unanswered questions surrounding this complex and unknown phenomenon.

It's Like a Giant, Complex, Unknown, and Mysterious Puzzle
The more you learn about Unidentified Flying Objects (UFOs) and Extraterrestrials (ETs), one thing is certain: it quickly escalates into a myriad of different directions, compounding itself into an overwhelming, mysterious puzzle. For those that have explored this topic beyond what's in the daily media, you've undoubtedly discovered how you can quickly go down the rabbit hole.

But, unlike typical puzzles, with this topic, you don't know what the final picture will be. You also don't realize how many pieces there are. And it quickly evolves into a kind of three-dimensional puzzle. Shortly after beginning to try to put some of the obvious pieces together, you soon realize there are whole sections of others missing. Continuing to learn more, some of these are discovered. Some of these don't seem to fit at first, but others fill in details that would never have been expected. Combined, they all eventually produce clear, but most unexpected results. Ones that defy what you think you know about basic history. Again, the real challenge described previously is simply to continue reading.

Despite what the evidence clearly suggests and how the pieces of the puzzle fit together, few, if any, will believe this. For most, this would require a lot research, and time to adjust to a new reality. And, by time, this is measured in years. I can vouch for this, having gone through this experience myself. Despite lingering doubts; objectively and logically, the evidence speaks for itself. The pieces *fit.*

As a result of revealing this hidden information, there's another insightful analogy with the UFO/ET puzzle. It comes from the Greek mythology of Pandora's Box. If you aren't familiar with this story, it's described in Google as, "...Pandora's box was a gift from the gods... It contained all the evils of the world, which were released when Pandora opened the box. However, it also contained hope, which remained inside the box."[1] Based on the findings outlined here, you will learn that this is a perfect description of the UFO/ET phenomenon in its entirety.

Once you begin to see how all the pieces of the puzzle fit together more research and time to adjust to a new reality. And, by time, this is measured in years. I can vouch for this, having gone through this experience myself. Despite lingering doubts, objectively and logically, the evidence speaks for itself. The pieces *fit.*

A Need to Know

This is about being exposed to and realizing a possible reality that society as a whole is completely unaware of, and, of enormous importance to the entire human race on Earth. It's a narrative that's entirely consistent with our own history of conquest and exploitation of other less technologically advanced societies. A theme that has continued to the present. Only, in this case, the advanced civilizations involved here are from other worlds. Ones that possess almost infinitely more experience and technology in pursuing these ends. And, as you'll learn, some have similar goals of exploiting us – like we've done to less developed societies in the past – for their gain.

And realize the most unbelievable aspects aren't what you'd think they are. They're not those directly related to UFOs or ETs, but coming from the

---

[1] Google search "Pandora's Box"

politics and our history. Read it like fiction, but understand it for what it is.

Pandora's Box Analogy
Once you begin to see how all the pieces of the puzzle fit together, you realize how appropriate the Pandora's Box analogy parallels the hidden components of the UFO/ET phenomenon. You'll come to realize the depth of the topic, as well as begin to uncover some of its secrets. With this, you're confronted with a number of concerns that redefine your appreciation of the value and importance of this topic. At the same time, though, there are many aspects of this information and awareness that offer hope.

What's really profound about this comparison of the topic of UFOs/ETs to Pandora's Box is that it is such an apt description. And it's not about the believability but about the secrecy, importance, and what it reveals. It explains what has been observed. Why history has unfolded the way it has. And, the events contributing to it that we are aware of.

It is an entirely accurate statement of fact based on all the information available. The pieces fit. As a result, this is no longer an academic topic. Learning more about this topic leads to political and economic realizations that redefine our society, with potential consequences affecting everyone.

Another Unfortunate Association
An unavoidable consequence of the information unveiled with this deeper dive into UFOs and ETs is describing it as a conspiracy theory. For many, this will be like waving a red flag. This is another compounding issue with the study of UFOs and ETs. It's inherent and unavoidable. Any investigation that goes beyond the surface will encounter this. And, the reason is simple. It's because the term accurately describes what the evidence suggests. This is just another challenge for readers to face. And, another reason to treat it like fiction if you have doubts.

An Inconvenient Truth
It's necessary to point out these problematic facts upfront. They are inescapable impediments to learning anything beyond the most superficial aspects of this phenomenon. The underlying truth of the UFO/ET phenomenon isn't a B-rated movie. It's a complex, dark, and sinister plot

that has many attributes of a political horror story. As you'll learn, this is the underlying reason for all the secrecy. In part, this is, in all likelihood, one reason why the news media avoids them. It's not what people want to know. The other reasons are – as you might guess – the direct result of the conspiracy to deceive the public. As a result, these attributes are also an unavoidable part of this book.

What I'm suggesting is even if you were to suspect the contents are accurate, you'll still have doubts. The findings are *that* astonishing. This is for several reasons. First, they completely upend history. They reveal an unbelievable covert plot of deception of immense proportions on the part of ours and other governments. This can jeopardize our faith in fundamental institutions, which threatens our society in numerous ways. And, finally, it's so fantastic it just seems totally crazy to all but the most open-minded or conspiracy-minded.

Direction
To overcome this inevitable barrier, keep in mind the goals: first, to learn; second, to gain a deeper understanding; and finally, to realize the importance of the UFO/ET topic in its entirety. While accepting the contents would be preferred, it is not necessary.

The Bottom Line
The belief in UFOs/ETs encompasses a broad spectrum, from those who deny any existence of both, to the few that recognize the reality of the evidence presented here, and are open to seemingly incredible conjectures. This is for all of you, regardless of where you fall on this scale of belief.

I hope you find this interesting and enjoy the journey into the previously unknown. One that has a strong probability of being real for all of us.

UNBELIEVABLE

CHAPTER 2 SECRECY AND DECEPTION

There's one simple fact that quickly becomes evident with anything beyond the most superficial and cursory examination of the topic of UFOs and ETs. And, this quickly explains the underlying reason for all the mystery. It soon becomes apparent that extreme secrecy surrounds this subject matter. Digging deeper, one finds it's to an extent that few realize. This provides a clear answer as to why there are so many unknowns associated with this phenomenon. It suggests why there is no physical evidence to speak of. And, it also reveals the UFO/ET evidence that is reported, has been consistently covered up, discredited, and trivialized. So much so, that it's often thought of as being *unbelievable*.

But this is just the beginning of this phenomenon. If most were to realize the extent and efforts involved to maintain this absolute secrecy – encompassing threats, abuse, and even death in some cases – they would face similar disbelief in it being also *unbelievable*. The overwhelming evidence clearly indicates that this policy has been in effect since the early 1940s in the U.S., or eighty years. Another *unbelievable* fact.

The Added Questions
With this realization, it prompts an immediate question. *Why*? Another is, *how* could this be kept a secret for so long? And, while many might think they know the answers, one of the reasons for this book is to expose some hidden ones that are overlooked. Another is to add to the appreciation of their importance.

Trying to capture the depth of all of this, is well beyond the scope of this book. As a result, particularly credible examples will be utilized to highlight the main points. The following example briefly serves to illustrate the efforts devoted to keeping anything associated with UFOs and ETs secret – in this case, by the U.S. Government. I chose this because of the indisputable source, the experience, and the commonality this has with countless others. In presenting this, I have two goals. First, to introduce an example of the credible evidence available. And second, to prompt further interest – if you have any doubts to the secrecy involved with this subject matter.

An Example Illustrating the Secrecy
Early in my studies, I encountered the book *Incident at Devil's Den* by Terry Lovelace, Esq., published in 2018. In this, he describes multiple life experiences he had - both as a child and as an adult – with UFOs and ETs. But, despite all of these and their significance in themselves, they are not unprecedented, nor the focus here. This is about what happened after an encounter with a UFO he and a co-worker had while they were serving in the Air Force in 1977. It's what

he and his friend suffered subsequent to their encounter that is of particular interest and relevance to the government secrecy of UFOs and ETs.

As a result of their *close* encounter experience and evidence, extreme efforts were made to try to cover up the entire incident. It describes how this only added to their subsequent trauma, with impacts on both of them and their careers, which ultimately resulted in his friend's death.

When you read this, it's difficult to conceive any of this as having been made up or exaggerated. Like much of what is presented in his book, it's impossible to convey the emotional depth without reading it firsthand. That's the only way to get a real appreciation of its genuineness and authenticity. As you'll learn, this isn't the only author I'll cite with this characteristic.

However, there's more substantiating that this is real. In this case, even more convincing is the author's background, accomplishments, and character. He is a six-year veteran of the Air Force. He went on to first get a bachelor's degree in Psychology, followed by earning a Juris Doctor Law degree. Then, he achieved a long and distinguished career as an attorney, both in private and public practice, and retired as the former Assistant Attorney General for the State of Vermont.

In other words, this isn't someone with any motive other than to share the truth. There's no hint or reason to present false or misleading information. Quite the opposite, as he states, he waited to publish this following his retirement to avoid jeopardizing his career. This risk was very real. Something that could not be afforded with the career path he chose. His goal was to share the truth.

As an author with the same goal, I can relate. As you read this book further, you'll appreciate my same concern with the startling and unbelievable findings I'm sharing. It's just part of the genre.

The Experience

In short, he and his co-worker went camping in the Devil's Den Arkansas State Park. During their first evening in a remote area, they were *visited* and had a close encounter of the third kind – meaning a face-to-face encounter with an ET and a large UFO. In the process, they suffered what appeared to be symptoms of severe radiation poisoning. When they returned to their base, they sought treatment. This triggered a sequence of events demonstrating the extreme secrecy associated with these types of experiences – involving UFOs and ETs.

The Cover Up

At the tail end of a week in the hospital recovering, they were interviewed by two OSI (Office Special Investigations) agents. This is the investigative arm of the U.S. Air Force's (USAF) Security Police. Being *interviewed* doesn't really describe this experience. Rather than being treated as victims, they were – in the terms of one of the agents – "in trouble." Lovelace was read his rights under the Uniform Code of Military Justice (UCMJ), as all of these were recorded by tape. He was required to sign releases and consent forms, among other things, giving them the right to search both his car and his home (which, as it turned out, was occurring at that time – the car, in fact, was confiscated). All of this transpired while he was experiencing continued severe pain coming from his burns. While literally being *grilled*, this was all under duress and pressure to cooperate. It would appear, from the line of questioning, that they suspected the two had ulterior motives for the trip, their actions, and were hiding film of pictures they had taken.

Another immediate result of this situation was being informed that he and his co-worker were being reassigned to completely separate locations. In addition, they were warned not to communicate with one another. Both had been EMTs (emergency medical technicians) working together as a team.

To compound matters, Lovelace stopped by his partner's home to say a "quick goodbye." This proved to be a major mistake, further revealing the extent of concerns the government had about this event. After about 4 minutes, as he and his wife were leaving his friend's home, two security policemen in a marked car parked in front of theirs. Another truck attempted to box them in to impede them from leaving. Despite this, his wife was able to drive home, during which they were closely followed. Upon entering the house, the phone rang with one of the original OSI agents who initially interrogated him. After a brief conversation of accusations, the agent hung up. These were obvious efforts to intimidate them both.

With his subsequent return to duty, Lovelace was reassigned to an abandoned garage to paint plywood in stacks. He was isolated during this duty. When he completed this task, he was then ordered to strip the paint off of each piece by hand using sandpaper. After two months of this, he was called back and given a ride in a military police car to OSI headquarters. He was then placed in a locked interrogation room and left to wait for almost 3 hours. The two original agents finally showed up. After some additional recorded questions, he was informed that he'd be hypnotized under the influence of a drug. The focus continued to be on photography, cameras, and previously discussed "missing film." This would change as the interrogation continued.

Evidence of the Government's Knowledge and Intent
Under the drug's influence, he was asked to recount his experience with the UFO and ETs. Having not been able to previously recall the experience after it happened, this brought it all back. It also triggered memories from his previous experiences with ETs. As it turned out, during this questioning, it became apparent these officers were already well-informed of the ETs and similar experiences. Lovelace also shared that on the UFO, he saw fifty-sixty

humans, some being crew members. He also saw evidence of human hybrids in aquariums. In all, he recounted numerous previous experiences as well.

He described the ETs as being from a distant system with two suns and moons, but they operate out of the dark side of the moon – their ship being so large it would be visible from Earth. He also told the agents about humans living with them on the moon. (These are all important details because they collaborate with numerous others who have had similar experiences.) He remembered and also revealed that he'd had an ET companion during all of these experiences. At the end of their interrogation, the agents indicated Lovelace would remember nothing. He was told to "finish out (your) enlistment and go to college... There's nothing on your record to worry about so long as you keep your mouth shut." Rather than forgetting, he had learned so much more, recovering lost memories and finding that the Air Force knew far more than they were letting on.

Years later, it was discovered that Lovelace had an alien implant in one of his knees. This is another somewhat common trait of people who are repeatedly abducted during their lives.

While there's ample evidence of many people with similar experiences, this one exemplified many of their common characteristics. It illustrates the efforts to keep UFOs and ETs secret. This program or policy has been in effect since the early '40s. By the 1970s, it was well-established and had a standard operating procedure. There have been many similar cases involving military personnel that have had worse threats and repercussions, up to and including death. This is no exaggeration.

The Obvious Reasons for the Secrecy
With further thought, some rather obvious reasons for this secrecy come to mind. These relate both to UFOs and ETs. It is useful to outline these components of the UFO/ET phenomenon separately at this point. On the surface, UFO sightings and experiences typically reveal technology that is far advanced from what our current science can explain, let alone create. This prompts security concerns with both the potential threat involved and

the advantages it would have if acquired. These lead directly to questions about the source of the UFOs and their intents.

Since it's unlikely this is human-sourced technology, it suggests an ET origin. Clearly, this only magnifies the same concerns with security, threats, and intents. It also raises a number of added issues, such as religious and societal anxieties, as well as human/ET relations.

These identify the most recognizable questions regarding the need for secrecy, but in fact, there are many more. These are the subjects of Chapter 19 and are actually what initially prompted this book. One of these was the result of relatively recent history and related unexplained events. This is where the most surprising evidence lies – that undermines what we think we know.

Summary
The point of this chapter is to explain why there's so little physical evidence. It's to explain the inherent doubt with photos and videos, as well as the testimonies of experiencers and eyewitnesses. It's to reveal the fact that there are still concerted efforts to cover up, deny, trivialize, and discredit anyone coming forward. Those who have, have been typically subject to ridicule, with their reputations being ruined or worse. Increasingly, whistle-blowers (previous military or government personnel) are sharing their experiences. In the past, most do so later in their life, where the previous threats are of less concern. More recently, due to some important new laws, current personnel are beginning to disclose what they've experienced and witnessed. In fact, Chapter 4 summarizes an important reversal with UFOs and a first step to this disclosure, resulting from a major admission by the U.S. Government. While this reveals important new revelations, it hasn't changed the overall official secrecy policy.

In short, there's a very simple explanation for a lack of physical evidence. It's all about secrecy.

Additional Reading for Those Interested in the Topic of Secrecy
Due to the inherent confines of this text, it can only introduce and briefly touch on the evidence and associated details involved with the topics being

covered in each chapter. As a result, at the end of some, I reference additional sources of information that I found particularly revealing or of interest. This is for those who would like to learn more about the topic. As an additional note, these referenced sources also serve as a small sample of the overall information available. They were chosen based entirely on my experience studying the genre, being particularly credible and authentic.

Additional Reference Sources

The book *Selected By Extraterrestrials* by William Mills Tomkins is an autobiography of a teenager recruited by the U.S. Navy at the beginning of WWII, who, having unique talents, became deeply involved with UFOs/ETs during his subsequent career, both in the Navy and with private aerospace contractors. It's referenced here to also illustrate the secrecy involved, the depth, and the accomplishments of a secret space program few are aware of.

Eyes Only – The Story of Clifford Stone and UFO Crash Retrievals by retired Army Sergeant Stone is another book describing the secrecy of the U.S. Government. His experiences are firsthand.

The book *Anonymous* by a nameless ex-CIA agent deeply involved with UFOs and ETs.

Alien Interview, edited by Lawrence R. Spencer, details the experience of Matilda O'Donnell MacElroy, a Flight Nurse in the U.S. Army Air Corps (WAC) in July 1947 when she was asked to accompany a Counter Intelligence Officer to a crash site to administer any emergency aid if necessary. As it turned out, she was able to communicate telepathically with one of the ET survivors. This prompted her to be involved in subsequent interviews. Some know the history of the many subsequent shifting explanations offered by officials at the time to keep this secret.

Another interesting book is *Military Encounters with Extraterrestrials* by Frank Joseph. These detail conflicts that still remain secret to this day. This will also be referenced later since it exposes a key event in UFO/ET history.

The title *UFO Secrets – Inside Wright-Patterson* by Thomas J. Carey & Donald R. Schmitt states this book's topic and why it's referenced here.

The book *Inside the Black Vault – The Government's UFO Secrets Revealed* by John Greenewald, Jr. is yet another with obvious references to the topic of this chapter.

Unacknowledged – An Expose of the World's Greatest Secret by Steven M. Greer, M.D. is another reference clearly reflecting why it's being referred to here.

One of the most prolific authors in the field of UFOs and ETs is Dr. Michael E. Salla. Each of his books reveal a wealth of information that provides insights into the depth and scope of this topic, the inherent secrecy involved, and the continuing developments that are occurring behind the scenes.

UNBELIEVABLE

CHAPTER 3: THE PEOPLE AND THE EVIDENCE

What We Know

Since few of us have either witnessed or experienced Unidentified Flying Objects (UFOs) or Extraterrestrials (ETs), what we do learn comes from other sources. If we were to have firsthand knowledge or physical evidence, we would know of their existence. But, without either, we are forced to rely on the *credibility* of people's testimony or what evidence might exist. This is where the *rubber meets the road* with the subject of UFOs and ETs.

Why is this different from other knowledge gained, where we take similar sources for granted? Do the differences make UFOs/ETs unbelievable or suggest another conclusion? And if so, *how* can we judge what is true?

These are all very good questions and the subject of this chapter. And, being literally the basis of everything most of us know about this topic, it's worth briefly reviewing.

Sources of Deceptive or Erroneous Information

It appears there are a number of reasons that questions surround UFO/ET evidence. The first relates to the previous chapter with government secrecy. The U.S. Government has a history of over 80 years of a known policy of denial, covering-up, deception, trivialization, and ridiculing sources of information or evidence relating to UFOs or ETs. In the past, they've even established committees, investigations, and subsequent reports further substantiating they don't exist. It's apparent that efforts included introducing false information to mislead – particularly to further suggest disbelief and discourage any interest in this topic.

However, other sources of hoaxes have been from people *faking* the phenomenon – for whatever reasons. Then, there are those exploiting this topic to gain followers online or on social media, gaining influence, recognition, and popularity with the hope of going viral. Some of these even include popular media sources who sensationalize, exaggerate, or present deceptive evidence to attract additional viewership for profit. These are often found on YouTube, other online sources, and even on mainstream television. It's surprising how otherwise respected sources have done this.

However, the questionable evidence isn't limited to this because there are also sources that appear to deceive. Some are suspected of being sponsored covertly by those with goals supporting secrecy and deception. (The underlying motives for this are the subject of subsequent chapters.) Others appear to have the same motives as other media – recognition, popularity, influence, and profit.

Inherent Questions of Credibility

Those who are aware of this know that questions pervade any evidence regarding the topic of UFOs and ETs. This introduces doubt into any information pertaining to UFOs/ETs. Thus, it requires scrutiny for those who seek the truth. For the naïve that aren't aware of this, *what you don't know, you don't know.* This results in many falsehoods being commonly taken as fact or the truth is denied. There's simply no way to know without further consideration.

Credibility Factors to Consider

The most important aspect of any information is: what is the source's intent? What do they have to gain? What's their motive? And, in the case of UFOs/ETs, what are they risking? Clues to these questions can be provided by the source. The media utilized provides some insights. Online sources such as YouTube draw immediate scrutiny, with the potential goal of going viral. This isn't to say they aren't legitimate, but it's a factor to consider. Another is the degree of investment required for the presentation. If it's particularly professional, where's the money coming from? This could be an indication of a profit or other questionable motives.

Related to this is: what do they have to gain? Do they work with, or are they affiliated in any way with the government, military, or associated contractors? These may suggest ulterior motives rather than sharing the truth about UFOs/ETs.

Another question is: are they exposing themselves to any risk? For existing or previous government employees or members of the military, this is a key question since they may be subject to prosecution, loss of benefits, including retirement, and even worse. And, associated with this is: what is their age? Are they currently employed, retired, or at an advanced age where they want to share the truth – with little to lose? These are added clues to the intent and circumstances of why they would be forthcoming.

Similarly, are the contents presented based on credible evidence from reputable or acknowledged sources? Are they based on personal experience, research, or solely conjecture? And, what is their background or knowledge base? Is there an underlying reason why they would come forward? What does their background reveal about their character? Are they *influencers*, *whistleblowers*, or those with knowledge based on expertise, training, or research? In addition to their background, do they have a past history with this topic that might provide additional insight into answering these questions?

Still, another quality to consider is whether they present the information in a balanced manner, considering all the possibilities, or whether they draw conclusions without examining any other evidence that might point otherwise.

And finally, is the information provided consistent with other sources? Are these other sources independent and unrelated? And, if so, what are the answers to their credibility? With more experience, you'll develop a sense of answering all of these. But, you never get past an inherent skepticism and doubt.

When it comes to credibility, I think of it as a *normal distribution*, where there are sources of fake information at one end and unquestionable ones at the other. For example, the U.S. Navy's accounts of encounters with UFOs on target imagining videos are pretty convincing. On the other end of the spectrum is the government's explanation of UFOs as being "swamp gas" when they were observed on radar. Most lie between these, not because of any intention but simply due to their innate uncertainty. This is just one added inherent element to the overall puzzle with the UFO/ET phenomenon.

The Resulting Inevitable Questions About this Book
At this point, you might be wondering: how does this book *measure up* to answering all these questions about information sources and their

credibility? Well, here are some answers.

First, I have no affiliations, relationships, or influences coming from any government other than being a resident, taxpayer, and voter of the U.S. My sole motive is to share what I've learned from investigating the UFO/ET phenomenon over the last five years. It is to inform you of my findings, which are both shocking in their content and importance. And, as I've already stated, the intent here is not for you to believe everything being presented. It's to increase your awareness and perspective.

As an engineer, this reflects my longstanding adherence to using the scientific method to solve problems. Only with this topic is it difficult to find ones with the ability to perform repeatable experiments. What offsets this is the wealth of UFO/ET reports; the accounts expose consistent results that are common and repeated with many observations and experiences. It's basically a modified form of applying the principles of the scientific method, but with the same validity to the results. You can't create controlled experiments to produce results, but the volume of experiences produces similar results – with the same inherent credibility.

The use of this approach, combined with the previously mentioned precautions or analysis of the evidence, adds further credibility to the contents presented. While some of it is certainly conjecture, it's based on this approach. And, what is, is backed by either history, credible evidence, or both. Nothing in here is the product of guesswork. Even the most incredible, unbelievable suggestions have substantial evidence to back them up. The findings are logical developments based on known history. So much so, that the one that seems the most farfetched is one I have been unable to come up with any other answers – as you'll learn.

Another common trait of the evidence I've used is that it is all based on – as best I can tell – people wanting you to know the truth. But, it's up to you to assess that on your own, whether or not you believe what's being presented. Remember, believing is not the goal here. It's to increase your awareness of the overall importance of the evidence. You don't have to believe it, to know what's involved.

Evidence, Proof, and Further Considerations

Despite all of this, or because of it, many still question whether any real evidence exists. The general perception has been that there is no *proof* of UFOs or ETs. And, as you undoubtedly know, *perception is reality.* While this may be both explainable and understandable, the reality is also that the belief there is no proof is both technically and actually incorrect. The following will reveal this by reviewing the definitions of *proof* and related terms as outlined. And second, by examining examples of actual evidence referenced in the rest of the book.

Definitions

These are provided for a common baseline for understanding the text material as a whole.

Proof – a conclusion backed by thorough research, sound analysis, reliable evidence, and a written proof statement or argument.[2]

Evidence – information or assertions that are relevant to the problem.[3]

Fact – a presumed reality – an event, circumstance, or other detail that is considered to have happened or to be true.[4]

Belief – something that is accepted, considered to be true, or held as an opinion.[5]

Truth – the body of real things, events, and facts.[6]

Know – to be aware of the truth or factuality of being convinced or certain of.[7]

---

[2] Elizabeth Shown Mills, *Evidence Explained: Citing History Sources from Artifacts to Cyberspace* (Baltimore, Maryland: Genealogical Publishing Company, 2017), 828.

[3] Ibid, 822.

[4] Ibid, 823.

[5] Meriam-Webster Dictionary, https://www.merriam-webster.com/dictionary/belief

[6] Ibid, https://www.merriam-webster.com/dictionary/truth

[7] Ibid. https://www.merriam-webster.com/dictionary/know

Credibility - the quality or power of inspiring belief.[8]

For many of us, this formal definition of *proof* may not be what we expected. Most of us assume *proof* to be a *given* – meaning something factual and beyond question. As you can see, this isn't technically correct.

Technically, this text could be interpreted as *proof*. I'm not making that claim, but it is a valid one based on the definition given by a respected source.

There are some key points here. First, *proof* is based on a conclusion, not necessarily fact(s). On the other end of the scale are those who believe there is no proof surrounding this topic. For most, this question has been answered with respect to UFOs. For questions concerning ETs, this is still open to debate. I think it will become evident from the information in Chapter 4, though, that this is a moot point despite authorities continuing to avoid acknowledging their existence.

Source of Belief(s)
So, what does this all come down to? Basically, a person's beliefs. Also, beliefs are often based on information other than facts or proof. It's important to note that while there are beliefs based on science, for most people, many come from other sources. (The belief in god is an excellent example of a common belief.) This suggests another is a *strength in the numbers* factor. Put simply, the more widespread a belief is by society, the more likely it is accepted. It's not necessarily the result of it being true or factual, but just a result of being generally accepted. For most of us – despite the logic involved - this alone adds credibility.

These attributes are particularly true of the topic of UFOs and ETs. There are a number of reasons for this. An underlying fundamental one is without an understanding of terms and the associated issues involved; there's no baseline for further meaningful discussion. This is why this is the first area of attention with the subject of this chapter (and the text), rather than directly answering the question *of where the proof is.*

---

[8] Ibid. https://www.merriam-webster.com/dictionary/credibility

Summary

Hopefully, this chapter has raised your awareness of the issues involved with evidence-based proof and how we all determine what is true. If you haven't experienced or seen it yourself, this is the real inherent limitation of the UFO/ET conundrum. But, it's also one that can be understood and addressed – if you have sufficient interest and an open mind. These are prerequisites for this topic.

Let the journey begin.

PART II FOCUS ON THE DETAIL
The Trees

UNBELIEVABLE

CHAPTER 4 UFOS ARE REAL?

Up until a few years ago, this chapter would have been devoted to presenting evidence testifying to the reality of Unidentified Flying Objects (UFOs). However, this changed with a New York Times front-page headline article in their Sunday, December 17, 2017 edition. This disclosed a secret military program investigating UFOs (in official terms, Unidentified Aerial Phenomenon, or UAPs) and presented unquestionable evidence of their existence.[9]

A Startling Reversal and Revelation...the 2004 Naval Encounter

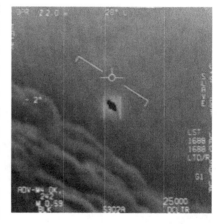

The 2017 article discloses an incident off of the San Diego, California coast on November 14, 2004, involving a U.S. Navy (USN) exercise. For two weeks, the naval cruiser U.S.S. Princeton had been tracking mysterious aircraft. On this day, "the objects appeared suddenly at 80,000 feet, and then hurtled toward the sea, eventually stopping at 20,000 feet and hovering. Then, they either dropped out of radar range or shot straight back up."[10]

Two U.S. Navy frontline F/A-18F Super Hornets, with the VFA-41 Black Aces from the aircraft carrier USS Nimitz, were directed towards a bogey in the vicinity of the Princeton. Their routine training flight turned into investigating a potentially unknown anomalous threat. Arriving at the site, they saw an object just below the surface of the ocean. Hovering above it was a UFO "around 40 feet long and oval in shape."[11]

---

[9] https://www.nytimes.com/2017/12/18/insider/secret-pentagon-ufo-program.html
[10] https://www.nytimes.com/2017/12/16/us/politics/unidentified-flying-object-navy.html
[11] Helene Cooper, Leslie Kean and Ralph Blumenthal, New York Times Dec. 16, 2017

Both aircraft's pilots and rear seat weapon officers reported seeing the object. When they approached it, they tracked it using an on-board infrared targeting imaging system. The previous photo is from the resulting video taken that day. (This video is available from numerous sources by Googling "2004 UFO navy images.") The craft then left, accelerating away "like nothing I've ever seen," the pilot, David Fravor, commanding officer, said.

However, one of the most striking points of this encounter is often overlooked. With the initial UFO contact being broken, the two aircraft were directed to return to the rendezvous "cap point," which was 40 miles away and only known to the Navy. Less than a minute later, they were told that radar had picked up the UFO there. By the time the two F-18s arrived, the UFO was gone again. It's one thing for UFOs to be sighted, but how did it know where the "cap point" was?

Follow-up
Interestingly, there was no immediate follow-up or investigation. The aircrews were subject to the typical ribbing, but their Navy superiors didn't seem interested. Fravor retired in 2006, and nothing really came of it until 2009 when a government official he declined to name contacted him while doing "an unofficial investigation."[12]

Perspective
Since 1967, the U.S. government had previously stated that UFOs "were not worth studying."[13] These investigations included Project Sign, which was followed in 1949 by Project Grudge, and then Project Blue Book, which formally ended in 1949. All of these earlier projects had one thing in common – ostensibly, they were searches for the truth, but in reality, they were part of the government's secrecy program to cover up and deny their existence.

This changed in 2007 when then-Senate majority leader Harry Reid surreptitiously initiated funding for the Advanced Aviation Threat

---

[12] https://www.washingtonpost.com/news/checkpoint/wp/2017/12/18/former-navy-pilot-describes-encounter-with-ufo-studied-by-secret-pentagon-program/
[13] https://www.nytimes.com/2017/12/18/insider/secret-pentagon-ufo-program.html

Identification Program to investigate aerial threats, including what the military preferred to call Unidentified Aerial Phenomena (UAPs) or just "objects."[14] This resulted in Luis Elizondo, an intelligence officer at the Department of Defense, contacting Fravor in 2012. Later, having left the government in apparent protest over the government secrecy, he played a role in securing the videos and the 2017 release of this encounter to the public.

Ultimately, this led to the Department of Defense officially releasing, on April 27, 2020, three unclassified Navy videos. One was from the November 2004 encounter, and the other two were in January 2015. These have been circulating in the public domain after unauthorized releases in 2007 and 2017.[15] This basically was an official acknowledgement of UFOs.

Why Now?
This is one question related to this reversal in policy. The way it occurred suggests that the government was put in a position where it had little choice. It's apparent that either the USN became acclimated to the occurrence of UFOs and inadvertently failed to prevent the information from leaking from the 2004 incident, or, it was an intentional oversight by some level of their leadership.

This, combined with the resulting covert investigation buried in a Congressional Bill that few knew about, eventually resulted in the videos being publicly released. At that point, *the cat was out of the bag.* In addition to the videos, the media had numerous USN sources that had witnessed the event firsthand. Denial was simply no longer a viable option with this chain of events.

Hidden Underlying Questions
So, after 80-some years of denial, cover-up, deception, trivialization, and ridicule by the government concerning the existence of UFOs, they are now real? What does this imply with all the historical evidence extending back

---

[14] https://www.nytimes.com/2017/12/18/insider/secret-pentagon-ufo-program.html
[15] https://www.cnn.com/2020/04/27/politics/pentagon-ufo-videos/index.html

to the beginnings of recorded history regarding the UFO phenomenon?[16] Particularly those in Europe in the 1900s and, more recently, all that has been witnessed throughout the world in the last 80 years.[17] Were they really all bogus?

And, if not, isn't this evidence of a covert program of government secrecy?

For the government, these are both obvious and undoubtedly inconvenient questions. And, despite this, they aren't getting any attention in the media. It seems to be focused entirely on the details – whether they're real, what they are, or whether they are known objects. With the original and subsequent release of Navy target imaging photos and videos, it's evident that there are actual, real, unexplainable UFOs exhibiting unknown technology. Those weren't birds or swamp gas.

A Continuing Legacy

Despite this, other images have also been released by government sources that seem to attempt to put this into question again. It would appear there might be vestiges of the old policy of secrecy continuing. This is further suggested by the Pentagon, stating most are "misidentified ordinary objects and phenomena."[18] This sounds like a continuing policy that's been evidenced since the 1940s, where attempts were made to lump valid sightings in with obvious bogus and explainable ones. Is this a continuing attempt to cast a similar suspicion on all?

A Shifting Focus

However, real questions come from the 2004 encounter and further realizations. One is the unexplained technology. Another is the UFO returning to the "cap point." How did it know where this was? With both of these questions, where did this knowledge come from? Regardless, the continued secrecy serves to avoid or delay these answers. This would be the next step in the disclosure process (the subject of Chapter 21). And it

---

[16] https://en.wikipedia.org/wiki/List_of_reported_UFO_sightings#By_location
[17] https://en.wikipedia.org/wiki/List_of_reported_UFO_sightings#By_location
[18] https://www.reuters.com/technology/space/pentagon-ufo-report-says-most-sightings-ordinary-objects-phenomena-2024-03-08/

hinges on the next obvious question: the existence of ETs.

Follow-up Questions
Returning to questions related to the existence of UFOs, *where do they come from? Who do they belong to?* And *where does the technology come from?* Most would assume - without knowing anything different – that some are extraterrestrial. Well, as the next chapter suggests, there are fairly clear answers to some of these. They certainly reflect the technology that is outside conventional science, and thus, it's quite likely it's of non-Earth origin. The principle of *Occam's Razor*[19] could certainly apply here as potential guidance.

But the real question is, *whose are they*? This is also the subject of the next chapter. You'll learn in subsequent chapters that domestic (meaning of Earth origin) UFOs have, in all likelihood, existed since the 1930's. This is contrary to common belief, but there's ample evidence suggesting this. In fact, several of the previous examples of sightings could be from an Earthly origin as well, as you'll learn.

Policy Shift with Implications
Until recently, the U.S. Government has had a policy of total denial of the existence of Unidentified Flying Objects (UFOs) and Extraterrestrial (ETs). So much so there's not only been a concerted effort to deny but to cover up, deceive, trivialize, and ridicule the subject of UFOs/ETs for the last 80+ years. One of the most fundamental foundations for this was that there was *no proof*. Well, now that has been overturned. Intentionally with UFOs, apparently, but also unintentionally with ETs.

With the release of target imaging evidence and the testimonials of the involved military personnel, we've been told UFOs do actually exist. What you're not being told is that ETs also exist.

So, where are these UFOs coming from? Are they the result of some secret military project(s)? From the information available, this is quite likely for some. But what about the consistency of the phenomenon going back as

---

[19] https://www.britannica.com/topic/Occams-razor

far as recorded history? In particular, what have the reported experiences been since the 1940s? Are these all bogus, with only recent incidents bearing any authenticity? I'll let you decide the veracity of that assumption.

If UFOs have been around for as long as evidence suggests, who created them, and where do they come from? It's doubtful that they're of human origin going back to antiquity. It's possible they may come from remnants of past civilizations on Earth. There's actually a lot of information suggesting that ETs may inhabit the Earth underground. That might explain their origin and answer how they could exist and not have to travel interstellar distances to make their presence known. Unbelievable, but a potential possibility to consider. But where did these ETs originate from? It all leads to real ETs existing.

Ultimately, if UFOs exist, it's difficult to explain them without an ET source at some point. Thus, acknowledging the existence of UFOs is essentially revealing that ETs are also real. You'll notice that the government's recognition of UFOs has also marked a subtle shift from denying ETs to professing their existence is unknown - another significant, although generally overlooked, shift in policy.

What Hasn't Changed
A prime example of where the UFO/ET policy hasn't changed is that no physical evidence of either UFOs or ETs has ever been made public by the U.S. Government. This is despite the fact there's substantial evidence that the government has retrieved both UFOs and ET remains, both in the U.S. and overseas. Even where physical evidence has been recovered by individuals, it always mysteriously disappears – never to be seen again. These policies haven't changed. As previously pointed out, physical evidence is very convincing if validated. The absence of it is often used to deny the phenomenon.

The UFO Disclosure
It's difficult to know why the government has reversed over 80 years of denial of the existence of UFOs. I'd suspect it's the result of a number of issues. First, with the conclusive proof emerging from the U.S. military, it simply got to the point where continued denial was countered by clear,

unquestionable evidence – both in videos and testimonials from personnel involved. Another potential reason might be that it's time, based on an underlying disclosure plan. There are key elements that suggest a plan of this type exists, with the entertainment industry's science-fiction introduction of ETs to the public. There are also incidents where rogue responsible elements within the military and government surreptitiously release UFO/ET evidence to inform the public. There may also be other unknown causes that remain unseen. Regardless, UFOs exist now officially.

It may have been inadvertent or covertly intentional. But, it's certain that it has significant underlying consequences that haven't been fully realized. With ETs, it remains an entirely different matter. The repercussions are still too formidable for this *next step* of disclosure (the subject of Chapter 21). As a result, regardless of the UFO admission, it just adds to the UFO/ET mystery since there are still a lot of secrets involving UFOs that haven't been revealed.

But, with all this, why the shift to saying "there is no evidence" of ETs rather than the previous denial?

Additional Reference Sources
Leslie Kean's book *UFOs – Generals, Pilots, And Government Officials Go on the Record.*

Thomas J. Carey & Donald R. Schmitt, *UFO Secrets – Inside Wright-Patterson.*

In Plain Sight by Ross Coulthart.

John Greenewald, Jr.'s book *Inside the Black Vault – The Government's UFO Secrets Revealed.*

Military Encounters with Extraterrestrials – The Real War of the Worlds by Frank Joseph.

CHAPTER 5 WHAT ABOUT ETS?

At this point, you've been introduced to the Unidentified Flying Objects (UFOs) and Extraterrestrials (ETs) conundrum, with the inherent secrecy involved and the challenges with the sources and evidence that are available. Throughout modern history, UFOs and ETs have been intrinsically linked. With the advanced technology evidenced by UFOs, the logical explanation has been they are of ET origin. Delving into the associated evidence, this is further reinforced. The thousands of encounters, abduction accounts, and history all support this conclusion as well.

With the official U.S. Government acknowledgement in 2020, the existence of UFOs – or, as they describe them, Unidentified Anomalous Phenomena (UAPs) – has been finally answered. Associated with this has been another subtle shift in public policy. Now, the government no longer denies that ETs exist; they are saying that there's no evidence of ETs.

Even though this is not true, based on scores of independent sources, this change is notable. First, it's unnecessary with the reveal of UFOs. But, since it has occurred, it suggests something else has changed and that ET existence is now a possibility. Not possessing evidence does not preclude the prospect of their existence.

Like the acknowledgement of UFOs, indirectly acknowledging the possibility of ETs prompts the question of why now? With the UFO reveal being the first step in disclosure, is this understated shift in policy regarding a predecessor to a subsequent disclosure of ETs? Numerous ufologists believe this may be the case. Regardless, let's return to the evidence that already exists.

An Example
According to one U.S. government whistleblower, there is confirmation that over 50 extraterrestrial (ET) species are known (this was in 1979). No, this isn't a typo or a false claim. If you don't already know this, it comes from an interview Dr. Michael E. Salla[20] did with a U.S. ex-Army veteran, Sgt Clifford

---

[20] https://www.amazon.com/stores/author/B001HQ3F6C/about

Stone.[21] In it, he describes a training manual covering emergency treatment methods for known ET species[22]. He encountered during his schooling in the U.S. Army for recovering UFOs. Not surprisingly, this is subject to the usual debate, with the associated denial and discrediting of it being authentic. And, it's only one glimpse into confirming the existence of ETs.

ET Information Sources
Instead of a primary focus on examples of sightings or experiences, with the depth of the information available, I will be referencing particularly notable sources. In most cases, these will be authors, but this also includes other specific evidence. What's provided here only provides a glimpse of what information is available. These are chosen to highlight the fact that real evidence exists despite all the efforts and claims otherwise. This evidence – that ETs are real – will include those from antiquity through the present. Each is summarized, with the associated references in the footnotes on the page below the text.

These aren't widely known. The government continues to express the opinion that there is no known evidence of ETs. In actual fact, there's considerable evidence of ETs, including having detained live beings, as well as recovering remains of dead bodies. So much so it's virtually unquestionable that if there was any other topic involved, there wouldn't even be any discussion surrounding this. It would be evident. But, like everything about this subject, that's not the case for many reasons; some obvious and others not so apparent. (All are related to the reasons outlined in Chapters 2 and 3, and the reasons for secrecy outlined in Chapter 19.)

Therefore, the question *'Do ETs Exist?'* remains, despite the acknowledgement of UFOs being a reality. And, like the previous chapter citing numerous encounters with UFOs, this chapter will refer to sources of virtually undeniable evidence of the existence of ETs. While there may not be any tangible physical evidence available to the public, that doesn't dissuade from the essentially irrefutable proof that ETs are real.

---

[21] https:// https://www.amazon.com/sgt clifford stone
[22] https://exopoliticsjournal.com/Journal-vol-1-2-Stone-pt-2.pdf

The following sources are in chronological order based on the ET histories involved.

Zecharia Sitchin - Author

Have you, like I have, ever wondered why gold is the monetary standard by which everything is measured? Well, Zecharia Sitchin provides an answer in his book *The 12th Planet*. Growing up studying Hebrew, he was intrigued by inconsistencies in conventional interpretations of the *Old Testament* with what it said. Learning

ancient Sumerian cuneiform also revealed startling revelations and confirmed his suspicions. *The 12th Planet*[23] is his first book in *The Earth Chronicles* series, which was prompted by his desire to find out who the *Nephilim* were. As he states, they were an extraterrestrial race that came to Earth from another planet, Nibiru, which orbited the sun. As it turns out, NASA is aware of, and searching for a planet that remains unknown and is postulated to have a similar orbit as Sitchin describes. They refer to it as Planet Nine[24].

The gist of the series of books is that the *Old Testament*, Sumerian, and other ancient records of the time describe history accurately, upending much of what conventional science describes as the origin of man. They also reveal supporting evidence that substantiates the existence of the *Nephilim* with Sumerian knowledge of our Solar System that didn't exist until recent times. If this didn't come from this extraterrestrial race, where did it come from?

The *Earth Chronicles series*, with millions of copies sold worldwide, represents the culmination of Zecharia Sitchin's 30 years of intensive research into the history and prehistory of Earth and humankind as recorded by the ancient civilizations of the Near East. Within these seven volumes, he is one of the few scholars able to read and interpret ancient Sumerian and Akkadian clay tablets. This presents indisputable millennia-

---

[23] https://www.amazon.com/Zecharia Sitchin/Twelfth-Planet
[24] https://en.wikipedia.org/wiki/Planet_Nine

old proof of humanity's extraterrestrial forefathers, the Anunnaki, who visited Earth every 3,600 years from their home planet, Nibiru.[25]

These are only a few of the multitude of books by this author.

Paul Wallis – Author
As a Senior Churchman, Paul Wallis has served for 33 years as a Church Doctor, a Theological Educator, and an Archdeacon in the Anglican Church in Australia.[26] As such, he's extensively studied the book of Genesis, which affirms that God made the universe, our planet, and us. However, in doing so, he uncovered various anomalies in the text that offer clues that we are not reading the original version of these stories and of our ET ancestors.

In his book *Escaping from Eden*, he reveals an earlier story of human origins, almost obliterated from the Hebrew Scriptures in the 6th century BC and suppressed from Christian writing in the 2nd and 3rd centuries AD. This takes you on a journey around the world and into the records of ancient Sumeria, Mesoamerica, India, Africa, and Greece. They reveal profound secrets with UFOs/ETs hidden in plain sight in the text of the Bible.[27] This is one of four books Mr. Wallis has written on this topic.

Michael Tellinger – Author
In his book *Slave Species of the Gods – The Secret History of the Anunnaki and Their Mission on Earth*, Michael Tellinger reveals the Sumerians and Egyptians inherited their knowledge from an earlier civilization that lived at the southern tip of Africa and began with the arrival of the Anunnaki more than 200,000 years ago. However, as sent to Earth in search of life-saving gold, these ancient Anunnaki astronauts from the planet Nibiru created the first humans as a slave race to mine gold – thus beginning our global traditions of gold obsession, slavery, royalty, and gods as our masters.

---

[25] https://www.amazon.com/Earth Chronicles Series
[26] https://www.amazon.com/Paul Wallis books
[27] https://www.amazon.com/Paul Wallis/Escaping from Eden

Revealing new archaeological and genetic evidence in support of Zecharia Sitchin's revolutionary work with pre-biblical clay tablets, Tellinger shows how the Anunnaki created us using pieces of their own DNA, controlling our physical and mental capabilities by inactivating their more advanced DNA-- which explains why less than 3 percent of our DNA is active. He identifies a recently discovered complex of sophisticated ruins in South Africa, complete with thousands of mines, as the city of Anunnaki leader Enki and explains their lost technologies that used the power of sound as a source of energy. Matching key mythologies of the world's religions to the Sumerian clay tablet stories on which they are based, he details the actual events behind these tales of direct physical interactions with "god," concluding with the epic flood--a perennial theme of ancient myth--that wiped out the Anunnaki mining operations.

Tellinger shows that, as humanity awakens to the truth about our origins, we can overcome our programmed animalistic and slave-like nature, tap into our dormant Anunnaki DNA, and realize the longevity and intelligence of our creators as well as learn the difference between the gods of myth and the true loving God of our universe.[28]

Other Antiquity ET Sources
The three previously quoted authors offer consistent histories based on evidence from antiquity. However, this type of information doesn't only come from the Middle East. An Indian publication, *Interstellar Flight Magazine,* has published an interesting article titled "UFOs and the Link to Ancient Indian Literature - A Deep Dive into Fascinating Futuristic Technology from the Past" by Brishti Guha and Indrani Guha.[29] In it, they describe several sources of UFOs and ET technology from ancient India.

Modern Sources of ET Evidence
More recent accounts similarly stimulate a lot of questions. The following references are just a few, but they stand out with their authenticity,

---

[28] https://www.amazon.com/Michael Tellinger/Slave Species of the Gods
[29] https://magazine.interstellarflightpress.com/ufos-and-the-link-to-ancient-indian-literature-ee51e5df4a8

honesty, and irrefutable credibility.

Matilda O'Donnell MacElroy, Senior Master Sgt, Women's Army Air Force Medical Corp, Retired

Lawrence R. Spencer, the editor of the book *Alien Interview*[30] , resulted from receiving a package of material containing a letter from Matilda O'Donnell MacElroy. The contents included notes and typewritten transcripts of interviews that she took as a Flight Nurse assigned to the 509th Bomb Group of the U.S. Army Air Corps in 1947. All of this material was the result of Nurse MacElroy accompanying Mr. Cavitt, a Counter Intelligence Officer, to a crash site in Roswell, New Mexico, in July 1947.

She was an onsite witness of the UFO crash remains and tended to the only ET survivor. As a result of this, it was discovered that she was the only one in the group that could communicate (telepathically) with the ET. As a result, she was assigned to serve as the ET's companion. The notes are a compilation of the interviews she did with Airl, the ET survivor, over the next several months. At age 83, Ms. MacElroy decided to go public with this sequestered information that she'd kept secret since 1947. You can't help but be impressed with both her accounts of events and Mr. Spencer's editorial abilities.

William Mills Tompkins – Author, Retired Navy Officer, Aerospace Engineer

In his book *Selected By Extraterrestrials,* William Mills Tompkins[31] describes his experiences being recruited as a teenager by the U.S. Navy through his extensive career in private industry working as an aerospace engineer on dark projects. Highlighting some of the most significant experiences provides some incredible insights. At 18, he witnessed one of the most significant UFO events in the early 1940s, the

---

[30] https://www.amazon.com/Alien-Interview-Lawrence-R-Spencer/dp/0615204600

[31] https://www.amazon.com/Selected-Extraterrestrials-secret-Nordic-secretaries/dp/1975944690/ref=sr_1_3?crid=17Z9G7KQPCSQU&keywords=william+mills+tompkins&qid=1698605261

Battle of Los Angeles. At this same time, he'd constructed a fleet of scale models of naval vessels. These were so accurate that it prompted an investigation into how he modeled secret aspects of the ships involved. Recognizing his talents, he was encouraged to join the Navy. In 1942, at 19, I went through boot camp and served briefly as an aircraft mechanic. But, after hours, (because of his abilities) he filled a secret role in Naval Intelligence, serving under Rear Admiral Rico Botta, who reported to the Secretary of the Navy at that time, James Forrestal.[32] One of his duties involved attending debriefings of spies returning from Nazi Germany. (More on this in Chapter 15.) Once the reports were completed, he personally distributed them to both selected universities and aircraft manufacturers. In 1942, Tompkins was initially flown by Naval aircraft to accomplish these missions, but soon became a pilot himself so he could perform them on his own.

The Navy spies flew back from Germany with unbelievable reports of Third Reich SS secret programs involving Nazi UFOs, beam weapons, and hyper-dimensional physics.[33] All were the result of an ET ally that they were collaborating with. Tompkins was able to assist with interpreting the remarkable reports with an ability to *remotely view*[34] the German designs.

Another report told of two concurrent ongoing UFO programs at the time in Germany. The one by the SS, but another one led by Maria Orsitsch[35], also known as Maria Orsic, a famous German medium who later became the leader of the Vril Society. According to the agent, she was 16 in 1911, and later she was instructed by ETs to construct a large spaceship and move

---

[32] https://en.wikipedia.org/wiki/James_Forrestal

[33] https://www.amazon.com/Selected-Extraterrestrials-secret-Nordic-secretaries/dp/1975944690

[34] https://en.wikipedia.org/wiki/Remote_viewing#:~:text=Remote%20viewing%20(RV)%20is%20the,and%20separated%20at%20some%20distance.

[35] https://www.amazon.com/Maria-orsic-originated-created-earths/dp/1300599375

her and her family to another planet in another star system.

Met with total disbelief and skepticism, Tompkins confirmed this with his own visions. The spacecraft was nearly a kilometer long and was constructed in German subterranean caverns in Antarctica.[36] This is where their UFO activities were located. In addition to this, the agent reported that some of the Nazi SS were not human.

Getting back to evidence of ETs, Tompkins also tells how he worked with a number of Nordic ETs during his years following the Navy. At TRW, his secretary – and others he had during his subsequent career – were determined to be Nordic ETs. The information Tompkins disclosed in his *Selected By Extraterrestrials*[37] series of books is quite revealing in many respects. What's introduced here is just a small portion. It's difficult to read his books and not realize how authentic and genuine his experiences are. As an FYI, the U.S. Government discovered this as well – with his reveal that the U.S. Navy had its own intelligence and space programs separate from the USAF/Army/CIA efforts. The latter were unaware of this reportedly until 2015 when he published his book *Selected By Extraterrestrials*.[38]

Michael E. Salla, Ph.D. - Author
Dr. Michael Salla is an internationally recognized scholar in international politics, conflict resolution, and U.S. foreign policy, having held numerous academic positions with multiple respected schools and universities. During this time, he has authored numerous books on these subjects. His last 20 years have focused on exopolitics – those involving ETs. Among these is his Secret Space Program series, which comprises six books that investigated whistleblower and insider  testimonies on multiple classified space programs. He is the Founder of the

---

[36] https://www.amazon.com/Antarcticas-Hidden-History-Corporate-Foundations/dp/0998603821
[37] https://www.amazon.com/Selected-Extraterrestrials-secret-think-tanks-secretaries/dp/1515217469
[38] https://www.amazon.com/Secret-Program-Extraterrestrial-Alliance-Programs/dp/0998603805

Exopolitics Institute, and his main website is http://exopolitics.org.[39]

As such, Dr. Salla is one of the most respected and prolific researchers in the field of UFOs and ETs. His books reflect a dedicated effort to share the truth about this intriguing and important topic.

Ardy Sixkiller Clarke, Ph.D. – Author, University Professor, Philanthropist, Human Rights Advocate

Ms. Clarke is an alumna, professor emeritus of education, and founding director of the Center for Bilingual and Multicultural Education at Montana State University, earning her Ph.D. in 1981. As such, she's written numerous texts, including a well-known book, *Sisters in the Blood: Education of Women in Native America*, which became a best-seller and is used nationwide in women's studies.

Her research has also examined PTSD, trauma, depression, and their impact on learning among Native youth. She is the co-founder of the Native Nations Education Foundation, which works for the rights of indigenous women and children in the America and South Pacific. Using personal funds to establish a scholarship program, Clarke continues to support the education of Native students by contributing 10 percent of the profits from her books to the scholarship fund.[40]

With this background and her Cherokee/Choctaw heritage, she's had a lot of contact with indigenous people, both in North America and South America.[41] Her talents, combined with her passionate interest in UFO/ET-related matters, have led to her authoring four books capturing firsthand experiences with UFOs and extraterrestrials. Lending tremendously to her credibility is that she doesn't seek out experiencers, but they come to her for her respect, confidentiality, and for someone to listen. She doesn't employ hypnosis or lead witnesses but simply records what they have

---

[39] https://www.amazon.com/stores/author/B001HQ3F6C/about
[40] https://www.montana.edu/president/extraordinarywomen/eow_profiles/clarke.html
[41] http://www.sixkiller.com/

experienced firsthand.

If you read her books, you quickly realize her personal involvement with those who come to her. This is reinforced by her commitment, which is demonstrated by her extensive career in caring. In many cases, she follows up with these experiencers for years to ensure they are doing well. She takes a personal interest in them.

The books are a compilation of individual eyewitness experiences. The mere volume of hundreds of accounts and the common traits exhibited testifies to their authenticity. I simply don't know how anyone, knowing her background, and reading her books could doubt the existence of what she describes from the eyewitness accounts she captures.

Notable Example
One of the most revealing experiences she relates is from a Bureau of Indian Affairs (BIA) police detective who encountered a UFO along a lonely stretch of highway. He was approached and invited into the UFO by an *insectoid* ET and asked how humans were uniquely identified. Happening to have a pocket fingerprint kit, he showed it and demonstrated its use with one of the many abductees on board the ship. Carefully diverting attention, he was able to retain the fingerprint he collected and later entered it into the FBI national fingerprint database. The young woman he fingerprinted was a 17-year-old from Las Vegas and was reported as a missing person by her roommate.

Additional findings from all of the experiences contained in her four books include the diversity of experiences and ETs involved, the suggestion of an alien/U.S. Government alliance in criminal activities, and substantial commonalities with these abduction activities. The majority of experiences recorded by Dr. Clarke are fairly typical of those found in other sources, but the number and obvious authenticity substantially support these ongoing activities and further their credibility.

Terry Lovelace, Esq. – Author, USAF Veteran, Former Assistant Attorney General of State of Vermont

The book *Incident at Devil's Den*[42] by Terry Lovelace, referenced in Chapter 2 on the government's secrecy of UFOs and ETs, is another impactful account of experiences with ETs. This example is again emphasized due to the genuineness of the account, as well as his credibility with the character displayed and his background.

ET Summation

Referencing these sources alone is insufficient to draw any conclusions for anyone who refuses to accept the possibility of life elsewhere. These are literally like grains of sand on a beach, with a vast wealth of experiencers – both from witnesses and abductees. As such, it only hints at the almost inexhaustible sources available relative to the subject of ETs.

However, the intent here is to illustrate both the volume and incredibly viable information available, providing evidence of the existence of UFOs/ETs and related matters concerning U.S. government involvement. These aren't meant to distract from all the other similar sources, which are in the hundreds if not thousands. These were some of the most notable ones that I came across in my studies. These were, in some ways, the most convincing due to their nature, the background of the authors, and their information. This will become more evident in the following chapters.

For most of us, ETs remain an unknown. This is just one of the many innumerable unknowns that still remain unanswered. Mysteries abound all around us with observed phenomena that can't be fully explained by current science. The UFO/ET phenomenon has a lot of questions associated with it. On the surface, and to most of us, whether ETs exist seems more like an academic question than one of immediate importance. As you'll learn, though, this is just another misconception imposed on us surreptitiously. As the title of the book suggests with the phrase *A Need to*

---

[42] https://www.amazon.com/Incident-Devils-Den-Story-Lovelace/dp/0578420325

Know, you'll learn why.

Acknowledging the existence of ET species presents an entirely different level of *Disclosure* (the subject of Chapter 21). One that unlocks a proverbial *can of worms* and is, in many respects, a *nightmare scenario* for the government and society as a whole. As Chapter 1 pointed out, it's a real *Pandora's Box* - one that also leads down a path that the dark government and the hidden economic and political powers want to avoid at all costs. Some of these concerns are fairly obvious. Others are typically completely overlooked. It's the underlying and hidden ones that pose the greatest threats. These are the primary ones prompting the extreme secrecy. This is due to it not being as simple as it might appear. These will be detailed in Chapter 19, *The Real Reasons for the Secrecy.*

I realize this is introducing information that, for some, is prompting doubt and disbelief at this point. The goal here is to inform you of information that you are likely unaware of, and how it is of significant importance. At this point, it's useful to understand why the answers to the question *Do ETs Exist?* are so profound, given the incredible information available.

WHAT ABOUT ETS?

Additional Reference Sources
Kathleen Marden's book *Forbidden Knowledge – A Personal Journey from Alien Abduction to Spiritual Transformation.*

Elena Danaan's book *The Seeders – Return of the Gods.*

The Ra Material – An Ancient Astronaut Speaks by Don Elkins, Carla Rueckert, and James Allen McCarty.

Stardust Ranch – The Incredible True Story by John Edmonds with Bruce MacDonald.

The Forgotten Promise – Rejoining Our Cosmic Family by Sherry Wilde.

The Secret Journey to Planet Serpo – A True Story of Interplanetary Travel by Len Kasten

The Allies of Humanity – An Urgent Message About the Extraterrestrial Presence in the World Today by Marshall Vian Summers

CHAPTER 6 ASSOCIATED MYSTERIES

In addition to the UFO and ET phenomenon, there are still some mysteries that don't have clear answers. Some are highly suspected but lack proof. Others do have evidence supporting their existence. And, still, others, with what we know or observe, just don't fit the UFO/ET puzzle yet. Some of these, which might be called peripheral phenomena, are addressed here. Despite this description, don't be under the impression that these are of lesser importance or impact. The issue of psychological influence may be the most challenging and important issue of all when addressing the topic of UFOs/ETs. The following will consider these phenomena in what I believe are their order of importance. This is purely from an objective perspective of a student, not someone who's experienced any of these firsthand.

Abductions & Animal Mutilations
The literal thousands of reported human abductions, combined with even more reported animal mutilations, suggest they are real. This is particularly true of the latter, removing any doubt that these are an all too often occurrence. With the animal mutilations, solid, unquestionable physical evidence exists. The question is: Why? Are they related? What do they have in common? Is there evidence this relates to ETs and possibly our government?

Well, from the evidence that does exist, it strongly suggests that their source is extraterrestrial. And that the objective is to harvest DNA. Some abductees report that the ETs involved have openly revealed their hybridization programs to clone or create new breeds of species using human DNA. Many abductees have been impregnated, subsequently become pregnant, and only then have no more symptoms months later – with their pregnancy disappearing. Others even have been abducted to meet their subsequent offspring and, in some cases, interact with them.

With animal mutilations, the laser precision of the removal of specific tissues implies several intentions for the removed organs. One explanation could be harvesting DNA, but other possibilities exist as well.

With animal mutilations, there's a related experience often reported.

Witnesses report sighting helicopters – typically black. This suggests the possibility of a cooperative effort with the dark military (or other organizations) and the exploitive aliens. This collaborative type of relationship is discussed further in subsequent chapters.

Of course, there are other more sinister explanations for both human abductions and animal mutilations. With the first, there's evidence of abductees being permanently retained, never to be returned. This suggests two distinct possibilities: slavery or consumption. With the latter, that might also offer another answer for the animal mutilations – maybe the collected organs are delicacies with some ETs. All of these are obviously sinister. And, like everything relating to the topic of UFOs/ETs, the potential answers to these questions remain in doubt, depending on your beliefs.

ET Communications with Channelers

There are numerous channelers who claim to have psychically communicated with ETs – both in the past and currently. Similarly, strong supporting evidence exists for this occurrence. One of note is *The Ra Material* by Don Elkins, Carla Rueckert, and James Allen McCarty. It contains the exact recordings of twenty-six sessions with an ET named Ra. It's the end result of nineteen years of research into channeling communications with other beings. It's the result of a small research group using a scientific approach. It's a very enlightening account of an ET with a particularly revealing background and knowledge.[43]

Another account of channeling comes from Elena Danaan with her book *The Seeders – Return of the Gods*. As an archeologist working many years studying ancient Egyptian sites, and with a remarkable background in spiritualism, she's been an extraterrestrial contactee since childhood. As a result, she became an emissary of the Galactic Federation of Worlds, the ET body responsible for regulating the portion of space that we inhabit. This is extensively the focus of Dr. Michael E. Salla's book seven of his secret space

---

[43] https://www.amazon.com/Ra-Material-Ancient-Astronaut-Speaks/dp/089865260X

program series *Galactic Federations Councils*[44].

Another of the most convincing – as mentioned in Chapter 5 and will be further discussed in Chapter 14 – is with Maria Orsitsch[45] (Orsic), which basically resulted in Nazi Germany's development of UFOs before WWII. As unbelievable as this may seem, there's ample evidence for this. Both before WWII and following it – particularly with Operation Highjump in 1947 in Antarctica.[46]

For those with further interest in this aspect of the UFO/ET experience, there is a wealth of books describing individuals' communications with extraterrestrials. Notable ones that I found in my studies came from authors like Elena Daanan[47], who's written several books on her contacts with ETs. Other authors include Lyssa Royal and Keith Priest[48], Jim McCarty, Don Elkins, Carla L. Rueckert[49], Lisette Larkins[50], Megan Rose[51], Sherry Wilde[52], and so many others that are too numerous to list.

Psychological Influence
One of the most intriguing mysteries relating to UFOs/ETs is the use of

---

[44] https://www.amazon.com/Galactic-Federations-Councils-Secret-Programs/dp/0998603880
[45] https://www.amazon.com/Maria-orsic-originated-created-earths/dp/1300599375
[46] https://www.amazon.com/Antarcticas-Hidden-History-Corporate-Foundations/dp/09986038216
[47] https://www.amazon.com/Will-Never-Let-You-Down/dp/B09FCHQHKF
[48] https://www.amazon.com/Prism-Lyra-Exploration-Galactic-Heritage/dp/1891824872
[49] https://www.amazon.com/Ra-Material-Law-40th-Anniversary-Boxed/dp/0764360213c
[50] https://www.amazon.com/Talking-Extraterrestrials-Transforming-Enlightened-Beings/dp/19379071391
[51] https://www.amazon.com/stores/Megan-Rose/author/B09NYLG9GP
[52] https://www.amazon.com/Forgotten-Promise-Rejoining-Cosmic-Family/dp/1886940487

covert psychological influence. There are two components to this: one, coming from the U.S. Government, and two, efforts by aliens to influence humans. The first becomes rather apparent with the extensive evidence and historical behavior exhibited by the government and the media to instill doubt, denial, cover-up, deception, trivialization, and ridicule with anything involving ETs.

A Suspected Influence Example
However, there are indications that the efforts of the government to influence citizens don't end with the UFO/ET phenomenon. There are similar hints that the government did fairly extensive research on this in the 70s. The best evidence is the apparent dramatic shift in societal norms in the last 60 years. Current politics are quite revealing in this area.

For example, the public reaction to President Nixon's involvement in the Watergate break-in and subsequent cover-up. Contrast this with the response to candidate Donald Trump in 2016, where he told Russia publicly he'd like to see them hack his opponent's email accounts and publicize them – which did actually occur. Nixon resigned. With Trump, nothing happened.

In the first case, the President conspired to conceal a theft crime. In the second, the candidate for President expressed his desire for an adversary government to electronically steal data pertaining to the election and release it to the Press. And, in this case, that's exactly what happened.

The ET efforts to influence human behavior through psychological means, remains unknown. As one might suspect, there appears to be no direct evidence of this existing or being used. But, even with this, there are signs it's been employed very effectively, particularly being suspected of having significant influence over politics. And, with the latter, this seems to extend back to before the 20th Century in Europe. In recent decades, it's become increasingly apparent in the United States with unexplained dramatic shifts in public opinion. The reasons for this will be disclosed in subsequent chapters.

One revealing information source comes from the book *The Allies of*

Humanity – Books 1 and 2 by Marshall Vian Summers. These focus on aliens who seek to exploit the human race on Earth. It points out that most ETs exert influence rather than resort to force. And this includes psychic means. The book is an expressed warning that Earth is one of the few remaining planets that haven't been colonized by selfish aliens. It's the real reason for the book you are now reading. You have *a need to know.*

Men in Black

The Men in Black is another mystery. Often, they show up on a person's doorstep following an experience involving a UFO. Typically, the witness or experiencer is then warned not to talk about it. The characteristics of the Men in Black can vary. Their name implies what they usually embody in appearance, but they've also been known to wear white suits or a dark turtleneck sweater as well. It's their facial characteristics and color that are distinctive. Frequently, they are reported as having the appearance of an Asian, but with a pale white complexion. This can vary as well.

Other traits can further differentiate them from normal humans. Often, they're said to talk or move like an android. This actually suggests their origin may be just that, an ET creation, similar to the cloned *greys* that are commonly associated with ETs. Another common characteristic is that Men in Black are seen with black sedans, often Cadillacs or similar vintage vehicles from the '60s. I know this sounds humorous, but it's apparently true.

They also can exhibit out worldly characteristics. In some cases, they vanish without a trace. Others, like the following example, definitely exhibit paranormal behavior. What to conclude from this? Obviously, it's difficult to draw any specific conclusions from the varied experiences that occur. One commonality is that the Men in Black appear to have the same goal as the government – to cover up any experiences and sightings. That would suggest the possibility that the Men in Black and the Dark government are working cooperatively. As Chapters 2 and 7 suggest, these two groups share the need for continued extreme secrecy of their existence and activities.

As a result, it can be inferred that the Men in Black are non-human entities. Whether they are human or ET creations remains in question. It's likely the latter, with the antiquated or otherwise strange behavior that some exhibit. A notable experience further supports this conclusion.

A Men in Black Example

In the book *Stardust Ranch: The Incredible True Story by John Edmonds and Bruce MacDonald, it describes an incident* in 2008, where John Edmonds and a neighbor were working together at his Stardust Ranch in Arizona one afternoon. They observed a black SUV drive up to his property. Two classic Men in Black suits got out and walked shoulder-to-shoulder up to the steel gate. This consisted of steel bars about 10 feet high. As they watched the Men in Black approach impenetrable the gate, John expected them to call out for him to open the gate. What actually happened was most unexpected. The two Men in Black simply walked through the gate. Both he and his neighbor witnessed this. As the two Men in Black approached them, they wore the classic uniform: black suits, dark sunglasses, and black fedora hats. He also noted the SUV had government-issued black license plates. And they had "pale and clammy" skin, like "uncooked chicken."[53]

One of the Men in Black then warned John to stop publishing information. When asked again, he repeated the same message as if it was a recording. They both then turned, returned to their vehicle, and drove off. Once again, walking through the gate. Another interesting point is that John and his neighbor were both cleaning firearms on a picnic table full of guns. Apparently, the Men in Black took no notice of this, let alone let it intimidate them in any way. Not typical human behavior.

If you read John Edmond's account, it's both shocking in many ways but entirely believable in the way he shares all of his and his wife's experiences. His book with co-author Bruce MacDonald is a perfect way to end this chapter, with all of the bizarre experiences. It's a lot like Ardy Sixkiller Clarke's books in that the presentation, authenticity of the experiences, and consistencies are quite convincing. Neither of them has any substantial gain from sharing this information. Their goal is merely to inform interested

---

[53] https://www.amazon.com/Stardust-Ranch-Incredible-True-Story/dp/0992132878

readers.

Crop Circles, Skin Walkers, Etc. Questions
Crop circles are well-documented and are known to exist. While there's a lot of debate as to their origin, some are suspected to be created by ETs. The question that comes out of this is: Why? How does this *fit* what is known? These are some questions that remain a mystery. Some are suspected of being hoaxes. Others, who knows? Maybe adolescent or rogue ETs are involved. This certainly could explain some, and there's reason to believe ETs exhibit this behavior, as humans share this trait as well. It's also possible that there are covert messages in some crop circles that we are unaware of. One of these could simply be providing an indication that ETs exist without specific evidence.

The multiple reported skin walker and related phenomenon are somewhat similar. With the animal mutilations, the sightings of strange beast-appearing apparitions, and ET encounters, no clear answers are available to explain these experiences. Like the crop circle phenomenon, there are striking examples of these occurring, but no viable explanations have surfaced as to why these occur. It's suggested that they come from portals to other dimensions, but these are mere speculations for real experiences without any firm evidence.

Additional References
The Forgotten Promise[54] by Sherry Wilde is an enlightening account of one person's experience with ETs and the associated challenges this entails. Starting with an initial abduction as a child, she's continued to have experiences with these ETs throughout her life – now being astral communications. This is just one, of many accounts where people have interacted with ETs during extended periods of their lives.

---

[54] https://www.amazon.com/Forgotten-Promise-Rejoining-Cosmic-Family/dp/1886940487

PART III REALITY AND IMPORTANCE
The Forest

UNBELIEVABLE

CHAPTER 7 WHAT DO THEY WANT?

One of the most surprising findings from the extensive study of Unidentified Flying Objects (UFOs) and extraterrestrials (ETs) is that ETs are like us in many respects. They are obviously more advanced technologically, as evidenced by their presence and observed behavior of their craft. This appears to be largely the result of their existence for far longer than Earth. Imagine if we were 1,000, 100,000, or even 1,000,000 years in the future. Think of the technology and capabilities we would possess. It's not like we'd necessarily be a lot smarter. It's just that we'd have advanced from all the knowledge gained over that period of time. Just think how far we've come technologically in only the last 100 years.

Further evidence supporting this comes from Dr. Michael E. Salla's books on exopolitics.[55] In reading his numerous books, one soon comes to the realization that politics outside of Earth is strikingly similar to our own, with the different perspectives and goals of the participants creating discord. This was one aspect of this issue that supported its credibility with me. ETs, like us, don't all agree.

But, as you'll learn in subsequent chapters, they've learned a lot. All of this appears to be supported by numerous ETs that are reported to have been encountered, the behavior they've exhibited, and their history with us. And, with some thought, it all makes complete sense.

A Common Goal
First, with the apparent considerable different ET species, it's important to specify the ones I'm referring to here. These are the corporal entities, meaning they are physical in nature, just as we are. This type of lifeform indicates they possess similar requirements to those we have. First, as with any lifeform, they are fundamentally motivated to survive. This is the most rudimentary and fundamental measure of success. Surviving for physical beings depends upon resources. In our case, we have a primary dependency on oxygen, water, and food – among other things. For ETs, these may be different, but it's probably safe to assume they are similarly dependent on

---

[55] https://exopolitics.org/

physical requirements for their lives as well.

The Role of Wealth

In a competitive environment, as we have on Earth – both in nature and our societies – species compete for limited resources since these are tied to survival. With humans, this competition is in the context of wealth since this enables the acquisition of resources and, thus, further supports our survival. Additionally, wealth is a measure of influence and power, which also ensures survival and heightens one's ego and prestige. These last two elements are one of the motivators for many of our world leaders. For many, wealth, power, and influence only whet their appetite for more. These innate traits are further, both rational and emotional incentives relative to survival.

It's evident that the more you study comparable ETs, the more you realize that some ET species exhibit similar behavior as humans. This makes complete sense and is entirely logical for these reasons. And, as the evidence reveals, it bears out. As a result, we can extrapolate what we observe from ET behavior to ascertain their motives – in other words – what they want as well.

And, like on Earth with humans, it's not what they say; but what they do that reveals their intentions.

The Two Basic Belief Systems

In studying ETs, we find their motivations reflect two basic fundamental values with corresponding behaviors. This is also evident for humans as well. One poses a threat by its very nature. The other does not, and in fact, can be beneficial for all involved. The first group exhibits values and behavior focused on opportunity at the expense of others. This describes *selfish* behavior. The second group can be described as *selfless*. These can be either benevolent or indifferent, but they have in common that they are not a threat. Unlike the *selfish* ETs (which I'll refer as *aliens*), they don't seek economic or political advantage from humans or the Earth's resources.

On the other hand, selfish ETs are similar to the similarly motivated humans we experience firsthand in our society. They want to gain from others. It's opportunity they seek. Whether it's individuals, organizations, or nations, it's the prospect of gaining wealth, power, prestige, influence, etc. And it's all at the expense of others (although they might believe and tell you otherwise). In some cases, everyone benefits. But, in others, the ones being taken advantage of are best described as victims. As you'll learn, often, the party exploiting others justifies this by suggesting it's also to the victims' advantage as well. An interesting concept, but one again, evidenced both in the past and present on Earth. Think of the 'benefits' the indigenous peoples or slaves in our history have received from being victimized. There's even still evidence of people claiming this today.[56]

The Potential Threat

So, we now have reason to believe that there may be *aliens* who are motivated to exploit others – in this case us. Possessing more advanced technology and experience, they are similarly positioned as Western European countries were in the Middle Ages. Spain, France, Great Britain, and the Dutch all competed for world domination by colonizing the rest of the world. What would suggest that this trait doesn't continue to exist with alien ETs, only on an expanded scale?

Fortunately for us, there's evidence to suggest these *aliens* are more advanced in wisdom as well. In this respect these 'enlightened' aliens have learned wars are extremely wasteful in terms of resources. Another factor in our favor is there are apparently rules imposed in the realm of our portion of space, with applicable policies avoiding wars, the use of force, or exploitation. Here's an example of where ETs – as a whole – exhibit more knowledge and advanced behavior than our species. This will be discussed in further detail in the next chapter, which discusses why ETs don't reveal themselves, and in Chapter 12, which discusses ET politics.

However, this situation just changes the nature of the threat. It doesn't remove it. (This refers to the previous chapter's description of potential unseen psychological influence.)

---

[56] https://www.washingtonpost.com/politics/2023/07/22/desantis-slavery-curriculum/

The History of Colonization
The comparison of Earth's current situation has other unfortunate parallels with European colonization efforts in history. Like Earth's population, the indigenous peoples weren't initially aware of the intent of those wanting to exploit them. And, once they were, they weren't able to successfully resist them with the colonizer's superior technology.

As a part of the interstellar community, we are part of a competitive environment for wealth. There are a number of concerns with this. First, we (the general public) aren't aware of either the existence of ETs or the resultant threat. Second, we're technologically behind as a result of the Earth having less experience. Third, we're inherently limited to the Earth and its resources. And fourth, as I mentioned before, we have little to no experience with this type of situation. All of these make us *low-hanging fruit* for potential threats from alien ETs.

(It's important to add an additional note here that it's likely this has changed somewhat over the last 50 years, with the possibility that several major superpowers have gained advanced technology from ETs – both benevolent and the result of alien trade. This is also revealed in subsequent chapters.)

We only need to look at our own history to see the probable direction for alien opportunists. When Western Europe was in its prime, the major seafaring nations colonized the New World. Their superior technology and diseases overwhelmed the indigenous peoples. The associated slave trade further victimized people of Africa and the Caribbean. As you'll learn, there's evidence of a similar pattern occurring today with ETs. The difference is that the aliens involved have learned that covert colonization is far more effective than one by the presence of overt force.

The Ultimate Form of Colonization – A Lesson in Exploitation
I gained some key insights into this perspective from the 2019 science fiction movie *Captive State*[57]. A most unlikely source, and the significance remained obscure to me until later when I was studying the UFO/ET phenomenon. It's a gritty movie about an alien presence ruling Earth. Here,

---

[57] https://www.imdb.com/title/tt5968394

exploitive alien ETs are exercising manifest control in the U.S. indirectly through the pre-existing government bureaucracy. Of course, they intervene with their own forces when necessary, but under normal circumstances, people are *governed* as they are now, with existing police and other agencies. As such, the citizens are fully aware of the ET domination and being colonized. But, at the same time, this approach has some benefits for both aliens and humans, given the circumstances.

The plot centers around a covert group of humans rebelling against the ET oppressors. Taking the concept presented in the movie one step further, my *realization* was: what if the aliens exerted their control covertly? In other words, instead of being visible enforcers, what if they remained unknown and their power rested on the exploitation of innate selfish behavior of the government/hidden wealthy elite? Rather than relying on open brute force, using covert influence that remains totally unknown to the general population?

Take this a step further. Imagine an alien colonizer who gains control through unseen influence. Say ETs have learned from thousands of similar experiences that the optimum form of colonization is where the victimized population is totally unaware of being exploited. First, by their being *in the dark* about ETs' existence. Second, by their naivety of Earth's value and position in the Universe as a whole. And third, and most importantly, by their political leaders – the result of seeking wealth, power, prestige, and egos.

Aliens initially approach susceptible leaders (those sharing their *selfish* values) and tempt them with sharing technology, wealth, and the resulting power and prestige. All this happens with the population as a whole being oblivious. Then, with this influence, they transition the human government to one of more advantage to them – specifically an oligarchy of strict authority, optimum manipulation, and minimum personal protections for the citizens. If you look closely, there's evidence of this happening – both from recent history and in the present. An unbelievable prospect, but one with clear evidence of it occurring.

Here, the only ones knowing the ET's presence and influence would be those with a *need to know*. Sound familiar? This is the guiding principle of the U.S. Government's secrecy program. From all accounts, this policy is what governs the current access to UFO/ET knowledge in our dark government. Coincidence, or a hint as to what's going on behind the scenes?

With this realization, my studies and this concept merged, with the recognition that there are parallels with our society, suggesting this covert colonization scenario is already occurring to some extent. This was the first significant *piece of the puzzle* that *fit* perfectly with the information I was gaining. As startling as it sounds, I'm convinced that this is partially in effect in the U.S. It explains everything being witnessed, both overtly and covertly.

This will be discussed further in subsequent chapters, but there are indications that efforts have been made in recent history to do this, and they continue today. I realize this: 1) it sounds like a conspiracy theory, and as a result, 2) it may be hard to believe. But it does explain a lot of what we are seeing politically throughout the world. It further explains the secrecy. It also is supported by considerable evidence, which is explored in the subsequent chapters. And, even if you don't believe any of this, it still explains why you have *a need to know* the potential for this situation to exist.

What They Want
To summarize, what some alien societies want is to colonize the Earth through the influence of those in power. In countries with existing oligarchs, this is relatively easy. With those such as the U.S. and other democracies, it's a little more complicated. They accomplish this covertly through the wealthy elites, susceptible elected/appointed leaders, in cooperation with industry and military leaders. There is also considerable evidence this is occurring today and has been in recent history.

Accomplishing this covertly, without the general population's knowledge, has a number of benefits. First, it's the most efficient means to exploit the planet. Humans, being unaware, are content and, thus, productive. And second, for the same reason, there's no resistance. It's a win-win from the perspective of those wanting to exploit the planet. Perhaps not, though, for those being victimized without their knowledge.

The benevolent and indifferent ETs either covertly assist similar selfless humans, or perform what is termed a *watcher* role of non-interference. And, like with the aliens, there's substantial evidence that this has occurred. This is described in William Mills Tompkins' book *Selected By Extraterrestrials.* Even though it reads like science fiction, considerable evidence suggests this is not the case. His experience in private industry – following WWII in the Navy – is working closely with Nordic ETs in his workplace. There's also evidence of other aliens working with other factions in the government.

There are others referenced at the end of this chapter for those interested.

Summary
So, in conclusion, we find that ETs exhibit behavior that reflects motives similar to those of humans. This makes sense since we all rely on resources to survive. With this theory, we can identify those who are *selfish*, the aliens motivated to exploit others. These are the threats. And, with their considerable experience and technology, they've learned to do this without force, with covert influence. Countering this are the regulatory bodies in our region of space. That, along with the selfless ETs, consisting of benevolent ones and those wanting to remain independent of Earth's affairs.

Additional References
One of the most profound sources of additional information pertaining to what ETs want is contained in the book by Marshall Vian Summers, *The Allies of Humanity – Book One.* It's the result of over 20 years of observation of the Earth and alien intervention. It's basically a warning to humanity to *wake up* to the threat. (One of the major motivators for writing this book.)

Beyond Esoteric – Escaping the Prison Planet by Brad Olsen.
And again, all the books by Michael E. Salla, Ph.D., detail the exopolitics that have existed in recent history. His books are an excellent source of information relating to this subject.

CHAPTER 8 WHY DON'T THEY REVEAL THEMSELVES?

This chapter returns to one of the most questionable hypotheses presented in the text. It's about Extraterrestrial (ET) influence over the human race. There are three reasons for this. First, it is so fantastic that most people would doubt this exists. And second, while there's evidence of it prior to WWII, there's less since. And third, what it suggests can easily be attributed to a conspiracy theory involving political bias, fantasy, or denial. Combined, makes it hard to believe. But, despite this, there's indirect evidence that it is occurring. Before this is addressed, let's look at what we do know.

Back to ET Motives...
In the previous chapter, we examined the motives of ETs to interact with Earth. We have the benevolent ones that have our best interests in mind. Then, there are the *watchers* or otherwise indifferent who basically observe what is going on but remain uninvolved and out of sight. However, we also have *aliens* who look at Earth and its human inhabitants as opportunities to exploit. We're all familiar with this perspective, as it continues to be so prevalent today with humans in our own world.

Once someone recognizes that ETs exist, it's not too much of a stretch to suggest that some may be motivated to profit from other less-developed worlds. This is a common theme with human behavior that has occurred throughout Earth's history, and thus, there's no reason to think it wouldn't exist similarly on a broader scale like the Universe – particularly given that some ETs are similarly motivated and the opportunities that exist. It all comes back to survival: wealth, power, influence, and egos. Some ETs may be more advanced technologically, but that doesn't infer that they are any more advanced in other ways or more benevolent. Survival and success still rely on resources and wealth in the physical world. As a result, we see the same two fundamental approaches to life in the universe as we do on Earth – *selfish* and *selfless* interactions.

As the previous chapter pointed out, many alien cultures, being considerably more experienced in exploiting other worlds, have realized that the optimum approach is to colonize them surreptitiously rather than by force. This is not only obvious, but it explains what we're experiencing. The evidence points to this conclusion and is supported by what we're observing.

With this, it also suggests that these alien groups would use covert influence to achieve their ends. There's an entire series of books on this by Marshall Vian Summers[58], titled *The Allies of Humanity*. In these, he describes how alien races accomplish their exploitation and how they attempt to gain our allegiance through influence, not overt force. Their intent is to exploit our resources – both organic and mineral – and not to waste them in conflict. In it, he outlines the four fundamental approaches. And what's really important is that with each of the following, you can readily see evidence occurring in the U.S. today. Again, these are UFO/ET *pieces of the puzzle* coming together to explain the observed behavior.

Influencing the Powerful Elite
Remember in Chapter 7 *What Do They Want?,* where I referred to the movie *Captive State* and how I theorized that the optimal form of colonization is for aliens to do it without the knowledge of the subjects? Well, in *The Allies of Humanity,* this is the first approach to gain influence over the world leaders, whether they are elected, other high-level government officials, oligarchs, or the wealthy elite. By *buying* their cooperation and support, aliens gain both their allegiance and control covertly.

Exploiting Religious Beliefs
The most insidious – in many ways – is the use of peoples' religions to subvert their values and beliefs. As Mr. Summers states, the aliens "understand that humanity's greatest abilities also represent its greatest vulnerability." Through psychic connections, they can impersonate spirits. As he states: "there are very few people in the world who can discern the difference." You can imagine how these aliens, with their thousands of years of experience honing these talents can be so effective in

---

[58] https://www.amazon.com/Allies-Humanity-Book-Marshall-Summers/dp/1884238459

impersonating religious Saints, Angels, prophets, etc.

Acclimating Humans to Their Presence

This is basically the second stage of *Disclosure,* as you'll learn in Chapter 21. We've already witnessed the first stage, the reveal of the existence of UFOs. In one sense, the *black government* is just going along with 1) the inevitability of the existence of UFOs being recognized and 2) the alien plan.

The evidence of this plan is apparent with the focus since the '50s on UFOs/ETs in the entertainment industry – both with movies and TV. By *fictionalizing* this topic, we all become unknowingly acclimated to the concept of their existence without the consequences of it being real. Then, at some point, when this does emerge, we've subconsciously been acclimated to it. The reality is less of a shock. Of course, this depends greatly on how it is presented – which will be of interest in the chapters on disclosure.

Infiltrating the Human Population

The fourth alien approach to gain control is to integrate themselves into the human population. This goes a long way in explaining alien abductions and all the experiences women report of being impregnated and having their fetuses harvested. It also *fits* with the male abductees almost universally reporting having their semen collected. There are numerous cases of mothers being allowed to view or visit with their alien hybrid offspring. The resulting blood relations build allegiance and influence that wouldn't exist otherwise. As pointed out by William Mills Tompkins and numerous others, ETs have been identified as appearing indistinguishable from humans. There are enough independent and credible accounts to believe this has been occurring.

Observed Political Phenomenon

To tell you the truth, I hate *going here.* However, if one looks at the evidence that clearly exists, it supports the elements of this chapter. There are simply clear indications that unseen harmful effects are occurring in our society. While they may be *explained away* or denied, there are sufficient indications to support consideration of external influences. As I stated before, if you can accept the reality of ETs and their advanced technology and experience, you can logically conclude they will use these strengths to their advantage. And, for those who desire to exploit Earth's opportunities, this leveraging of influence makes complete sense.

Chapter 12 is going to address world politics and related events from a historical perspective. Here, though, the principal focus is on recent politics in the U.S. – although I suspect similar occurrences have been observed throughout the world. I'll start by contrasting two similar events involving previous Presidents.

The Watergate Scandal
The first involves the Nixon Administration from 1972-1974. If you know recent U.S. history, you know President Richard M. Nixon resigned as a result of the Watergate scandal[59] involving his participation in the cover-up and interference with subsequent investigations of the break-in and burglary of the Democratic National Committee headquarters in Washington, D.C., at the Watergate Office Building. Following extensive investigations and revelations, Nixon resigned under threat of Impeachment. All of this caused a national uproar and a Constitutional crisis within the U.S. political system. For almost everyone, the mention of *Watergate* refers to this unprecedented public scandal – the Watergate Hotel, where it occurred.

It was never established if the break-in directly involved Nixon, but it was proven beyond any doubt that he directed the attempts to cover up and deny any involvement. He was recorded on tape having done such.

So, in summary, we had a coordinated effort involving the White House to break in and steal documents from their opposing political group. As a result of the following cover-up by the then President of the United States, he was forced to resign under threat of prosecution.

Request to Russia to Retrieve Emails
Now, fast forward 50 years to 2015, when Donald Trump, the Republican Party candidate, was running against Hillary Clinton of the Democratic Party

---

[59] https://en.wikipedia.org/wiki/Watergate_scandal

for the Presidency. During a nationally publicized news conference on July 27, 2016, he stated: "Russia, if you're listening, I hope you're able to find the 30,000 emails that are missing; I think you will probably be rewarded mightily by our press."[60] PBS News Hour later reported: "Russian officials began to target email addresses associated with Hillary Clinton's personal and campaign offices "on or around" the same day Donald Trump called on Russia to find emails that were missing from her personal server, according to a new indictment from Special Counsel Robert Mueller."[61]

"Russian actors sent phishing emails to accounts at a domain used by Clinton's personal office. They also targeted 76 email addresses on the domain used by the Clinton campaign."[62] "Mueller's indictment details a sophisticated, large-scale hacking effort by 12 Russian officers to interfere with the 2016 elections by stealing documents from private servers and staging their release through fake online personas...."[63]

"Later Tuesday afternoon, Trump's campaign tried to clarify his statements. Jason Miller, Trump's communications adviser, tweeted to say Trump was not calling for Russia to hack Clinton but to hand over emails to the FBI if they had them."[64] "To be clear, Mr. Trump did not call on, or invite, Russia or anyone else to hack Hillary Clinton's e-mails today," he wrote in a series of tweets. "Trump was clearly saying that if Russia or others have Clinton's 33,000 illegally deleted emails, they should share them."[65]

As a result, there were a lot of denials and statements by others – including Vice President Pence – trying to divert attention from the original request.

Let's analyze what candidate Trump said in his own words. First, by saying, "Russia, if you're listening," he unquestionably directed his message to a known foreign adversary. Second, "I hope you're able to find the 30,000 emails" clearly states a desire to obtain these electronic documents. Third,

---

[60] https://www.pbs.org/newshour/politics/trump-asked-russia-to-find-clintons-emails-on-or-around-the-same-day-russians-targeted-her-accounts
[61] Ibid.
[62] Ibid.
[63] Ibid.
[64] https://www.politico.com/story/2016/07/trump-putin-no-relationship-226282
[65] Ibid.

saying, "You will probably be rewarded mightily by our press," is clearly a suggestion to release them to the public. Now, what do we have here? A request to a foreign government to basically access these electronic records, steal them, and then release them indirectly to the public. Remember, this is all while he's running for the Office of the Presidency.

As a candidate for office, Mr. Trump is committing treason in soliciting a foreign government's assistance in subverting the Constitutional election process. Both were involved in the theft of documents, but only at Trump's request did it involve a foreign government. This is exactly what occurred. Russia hacked Ms. Clinton's emails and released them to the public through intermediaries.

What's different here, though, is candidate Trump escaped without being held accountable for any of this. And, went on to be elected with further help from Russia and other adversary governments.

What the ...?
How does one explain the contrast of these two events, separated by only 50 years? Was it a shift in moral and ethical values? Technology? Political changes? And, if so, what brought this about? There's no doubt that all of these played a role. Still, I don't find any answers to this when examining the high points during this period. There's clearly been a major shift in values and ethical standards, and/or, there are unseen influences undermining these.

Intervening Events
In mid-1971, the *Pentagon Papers*[66] revealed top-secret information redefining the reasons and causes of the Vietnam War to the public. It exposed the real intent of the government to deceive and exploit the public. The New York Times said that the *Pentagon Papers* had demonstrated, among other things, that Lyndon B. Johnson's administration had "systematically lied, not only to the public but also to Congress."[67]

---

[66] https://en.wikipedia.org/wiki/Pentagon_Papers
[67] https://en.wikipedia.org/wiki/Pentagon_Papers

In 1997, it was revealed that then-President Clinton was involved in a sex scandal with a White House intern, Monica Lewinsky. Adding to this was the President's denial, which resulted in charges of perjury.

Other significant experiences possibly impacting public confidence were the intervening 911 Attacks, the two wars with Iraq, and the war in Afghanistan – which only ended in 2020 with a withdrawal negotiated by previous President Trump.

All during this timeframe of 50 years, the country transitioned to the electronic information age with the advent of the internet and social media – particularly facilitated by the emergence of a widespread reliance on the use of cell phones for news and personal communications.

A Return to the Original Suspect – Alien Influence
I know this is quite a jump, but at the same time, it makes a lot of sense. How could we go from a society in the 1970s, where a divorce would spell the doom of a Presidential candidacy, to 2016, when a known divorcee and an accused rapist were elected? Similarly, when a President's involvement in a cover-up led to his leaving office, to one where a clear case of treason occurred without any follow-up? This is quite a change in ethical and legal standards. It's just too much of a jump for me to understand without some additional underlying reasons.

It's known that the President was elected that year by less than 25% of eligible voters. So, why did roughly 50% of those qualified choose not to vote? It's been well established that social media and foreign involvement persuaded them that it wasn't necessary since the Democratic candidate was portrayed to win by a wide margin. Is this a coincidence? Did it just happen? It is known that certain foreign adversaries of the U.S. certainly favored the Republican candidate for obvious reasons.

What's really difficult for me to understand, though, is how many of the Christian faiths have expressed support for the 2016 President-elect, with the known – questionable at best – characteristics he embodies. He is known to have avoided the draft during the Vietnam War. Again, he's been accused by multiple women of being assaulted, even raped. "A leaked recording from 2005 ... revealed him bragging in vulgar terms about using his fame to make sexual advances on women. In the tape, first obtained by the Washington Post and originally filmed by Access Hollywood, he makes lewd comments about grabbing women..."[68] by their privates.

What explains this unbelievable transition in ethics and values? Particularly among those who express the most devotion to ethical and moral values? How have we as a nation gone from despising unacceptable behavior to it being apparently embraced as a norm and of no consequence?

The Christian Connection

It's known that Mr. Trump has received substantial support from the evangelical community of the Christian faith in the U.S. What explains this? The authority of the Bible as God's revelation to humanity is their embodying principle. How is this consistent with their values? The only answer I can find references back to Marshall Vian Summers's[69]book titled *The Allies of Humanity,* where he states aliens exploit emerging races such as ours by victimizing the faithful through their religion. How else can you avoid the inherent contradiction in values exhibited by this?

A Potentially Related Experience

At one point in my career, I attended a meeting consisting of an audience of several hundred people. They were representative of a cross-section of workers coming from one industry. The featured speaker was a recognized hypnotist. During his presentation, he hypnotized a portion of the attendees – probably about 10% or so. None of the audience was aware that this was part of his agenda or was occurring. This was subsequently demonstrated by requesting those who were affected to come up to the stage. There, he asked them to perform functions they normally would never have done of their own volition. I knew several of these individuals personally, and I discussed this experience with them later.

None were aware of this occurring during the presentation. And when they

---

[68] https://www.theguardian.com/us-news/video/2016/oct/08/donald-trumps-sex-boasts-when-you-are-a-star-they-let-you-do-anything-video
[69] https://www.amazon.com/Allies-Humanity-Book-Marshall-Summers/dp/1884238459

were informed of what they did, they were quite surprised. It wasn't embarrassing, but that didn't dampen the surprise that they were hypnotized and performed the actions requested.

Conjecture as a Solution to This Mystery

What if, with advanced alien technology, they have the ability to influence a portion of the population similarly to the one mentioned above? In the years following WWII, both the Soviet Union and the U.S. invested heavily in psychic weapons-related research. There is extensive evidence of this with *remote viewing,* where individuals are able to view situations from great distances. One of the sources of this is the respected author Steven M. Greer, M.D. His personal experience has encountered psychic attacks. Working together in a small office, he and his administrative assistant both got a most unusual form of melanoma cancer. He survived, she didn't. All of these were efforts to silence their efforts to expose the secrets relative to UFOs, ETs, and the U.S. Government's activities.

Direct evidence doesn't exist, but there are significant indications that the Earth's population has been the target of *alien* influence. If you examine the motivations, the technology, and the subsequent behaviors, the observed results make sense. Otherwise, they are counter to what any reasonable person would believe. All you have to do is look at these actions in contrast to recent history.

Conclusion

Admittedly, all of this is based on more conjecture, given the otherwise inexplicable behavior witnessed over the period in question. I know it's simply too much to expect any reasonable person to buy into this, but I do think it's important to share. If nothing else, to provide you, the reader, with something to think about. Something to add to your perspective when viewing the media and other information. If this is upsetting to your beliefs, then I ask you to ignore it and move on to the next chapter. Unfortunately, this is just an introduction to matters involving more distress. Next, we're going to address the strong likelihood that the history we've been taught is false and meant to deceive.

CHAPTER 9 ET INFLUENCE, EXPLOITATION, AND HELP

Surprisingly, it turns out that *all* Extraterrestrials (ETs) have the same overriding objective: that of remaining unknown to Earth's human society. And, as you'll learn, this makes complete sense, whether they're *selfish* or *selfless,* as identified in the previous chapter. For the *selfish* aliens, if they were discovered, it would seriously jeopardize – if not remove – their ability to exploit Earth and its human inhabitants. For the *selfless* – both the benevolent and watchers – experience has shown that revealing the presence of ET species to less-developed societies can have catastrophic effects. Thus, all ETs share the common goal of remaining unknown to humans.

A Lesson in Exploitation
In the movie *Captive State*[70]*,* as mentioned previously, you see a scenario of Earth being colonized by an alien species. Only they did not take over the Earth as Western Europeans did in the Americas. They still did it by the threat of force, but they rule through the pre-existing governments – under the pretense of their original legitimacy. Definitely a more advanced and efficient approach. But, as the movie plot reveals, it still faces a major challenge in the form of the inevitable resistance from portions of the population.

Take this a step further. Imagine an alien colonizer who gains control through unseen influence. Say ETs have learned from thousands of years and similar experiences that the optimum form of colonization is where the victimized population is totally unaware of being exploited, first, by their being *in the dark* about ET's existence., and second, by the naïve belief of their planet's being the sole life in the universe. Third, and most importantly, by their opportunistic selfish political leaders, they seek wealth, power, prestige, and egos – which the exploitive aliens are all too willing to provide.

With this realization, my studies and this concept merged, with the recognition that there's a lot of evidence that this covert colonization

---

[70] https://www.imdb.com/title/tt5968394/

scenario has already occurred to some extent (as you'll learn). This was the first significant *piece of the puzzle* that *fit* perfectly with the information I was gaining. As startling as it sounds, I'm convinced that this is our current state of affairs in the U.S. It explains everything being witnessed, both overtly and covertly.

This produces the obvious answer to the question: *Why Don't They Reveal Themselves?* The remaining unknown eliminates several crucial concerns. One, there's no rebellion against someone or something that doesn't exist. Two, people aren't *enslaved* if they are totally unaware of it. Remember, *perception is reality.* Put simply, this approach to colonization is brilliant. The victims are completely unaware of it. The wealthy elites are reaping all the benefits from it, so they're content. And the aliens are similarly gaining the spoils. And, as you'll learn, they can even justify it on altruistic terms – being in the overall best interests of humanity. It's simply the optimum form of exploitation – a win-win, so to speak if you ignore the impact on the rest of society being victimized.

With this realization, you can understand the extreme commitment of exploitive ETs, the dark government, and the controlling wealthy elite to complete and utter secrecy regarding UFOs/ETs. It's literally the foundation of their mutual profit machine. And, as you'll learn in subsequent chapters, about the close alliances of these parties.

The Benevolent & Isolationist ETs
Both benevolent and indifferent ETs have a couple of reasons that remain unknown as well. These both relate directly to their benign objectives. Neither of these ET groups desire to upset, disrupt, or cause any damage to Earth or its inhabitants. Experience has shown that introducing the presence of ETs in some societies has resulted in total destruction. It resulted in internal disruption and conflict that culminated in annihilation. This is entirely counter to any selfless ETs' interests or desires.

Those who want to help the human race on Earth also want to avoid this at all costs. Even ETs who don't want to interfere one way or – by definition – don't want their presence to be known. Both of these selfless ET groups undoubtedly possess similar extensive experience and have learned this.

They know that's exactly what would occur if their presence were to become public. Chapter 19, *The Real Reasons for the Secrecy,* Identifies the multiple effects this would have on our society. No one wins with the existence of ETs being exposed prematurely.

However, there's an additional complicating factor, even if they want to communicate their presence publicly openly. The Earth is governed by multiple entities. They could reveal themselves to the United Nations (UN), but that would be extremely complicated and of questionable effectiveness. All of these reasons combined preclude any prudent public interaction. It would be too devastating to society at large, with all the different countries involved.[71]

Advanced Societies
As you would expect with their extensive experience, ETs have also *outgrown* some of the major pitfalls that the human race still struggles with. First, they've come to realize that win-win relationships are the most efficient and beneficial to all the stakeholders involved. This is a lesson that our *opportunistic* leaders on Earth have difficulty with. We seem to have a culture of win-lose ingrained with the associated ego-driven motives.

As a result, wars are disasters for all of the parties involved with the suffering, killing, destruction, and insane waste of resources. But that doesn't stop us from resorting to this in resolving conflicts. Based on what I've read, ETs do have to occasionally resort to violent conflict. However, under the auspices of the Galactic Federation of Worlds,[72] virtually all competition is accomplished through influence. This is psychological warfare that is unseen by the victims. It's my opinion that this is readily apparent in our society and has been for some time. This is also a subject for subsequent chapters.

Summary
Now we have a completely logical explanation to the question: *Why Don't*

---

[71] https://www.amazon.com/Allies-Humanity-Book-Marshall-Summers/dp/18842384591
[72] https://www.amazon.com/Galactic-Federations-Councils-Secret-Programs/dp/0998603880

They Reveal Themselves? One that *fits* the UFO/ET puzzle perfectly. It's for you to decide whether this is credible. If your knowledge about this topic comes from popular sources like social media, the answers provided are undoubtedly a stretch at best. Given the information available from deeper studies, it's literally quite obvious. All the available evidence points to this. This explains what is both overtly and covertly known about this topic. But again, it's all based on one's beliefs. The only evidence is revealed with further study, which takes time, effort, and a strong interest and desire to learn.

The goal here is awareness. It's a *need to know* and your choice what to do with it.

UNBELIEVABLE

CHAPTER 10 THE TECHNOLOGY

When it comes to the topic of Unidentified Flying Objects (UFOs) and Extraterrestrials (ETs), much of the immediate attention is often on questions of whether they're real, where they come from, who they are, what they want, the unexplained phenomena, etc. These have been the subjects of the previous chapters. And, while all of these questions are valid and important, they can divert from the overall importance of the technology. Here, it's easy to get distracted.

It's All About the Technology
Underlying all this is – the real substance and value – it's virtually all about the technology. History has shown that societies possessing superior technology can both dominate and profit from those who don't. With the realities revealed in Chapter 7, aliens seeking this have a clear upper hand. Thus, anyone with any knowledge *or* stake in the outcome will value acquiring ET technology above all else. It's all about survival. And as you learned previously, it involves wealth, control, prestige, and ego. ET technology is at the core of all of these. Thus, the real focus of the military, governments, and industry leaders (the hidden wealthy elite) is on gaining access to advanced ET technology. Thus, it's valued above all else for obvious reasons.

Associated Secrecy
With this understanding, it's easy to assume that technology is at the core of the secrecy. And national security does drive much of the need for this. But, the technology also has similar threats and opportunities to our economy as well (the subject of the next chapter). These, along with the histories of the subsequent actions of the parties involved, all contribute to it as well. These are the hidden aspects of secrecy.

One of the factors involved in the latter is how the technology is acquired. Some have been by force. Others, by opportunities. And finally, the most insidious, by trade agreements. Trade by profit or, in the case of agreements, by concessions. The chapter on politics will summarize these – based on the information available.

So, to understand this underlying importance, let's examine the elements of the UFO/ET technology – which is an extensive topic in itself.

Physical Phenomena

Both UFOs and ETs commonly demonstrate behavior that defies our normal science. Unlike typical aircraft, UFOs do not rely on atmospheric lift. As such, they come in a multitude of configurations that quickly define them as UFOs. Additionally, the behaviors displayed similarly differentiate themselves from conventional aircraft. Often, they are seen silently hovering, traveling at low speeds, or quickly vanishing – exhibiting unearthly speed – into the distance or space. Others, known as Unidentified Submersible Objects (USOs), disappear or emerge from the water, and similarly present speeds current technology can't explain. One of the most perplexing abilities of many UFOs is to reveal high accelerations that defy the laws of current science.

Similarly, ET experiencers report phenomena that are also outside the realm of known science. These include consistent multiple reports of abilities to *walk through walls*, levitation, and transparent metal. (The latter used to be science fiction; it is now science fact.)[73]

Suspected ET Technologies

It's interesting to examine the timing of suspected UFO retrievals and subsequent innovations in recent decades. There's a lot of evidence that UFOs were recovered beginning in the early 1940s. There are sources that state three UFOs were acquired in 1947. There's also information from quite credible sources that these were reverse-engineered by domestic manufacturers to uncover new technologies.[74] The developments in the following years are remarkable. These include solid-state electronics, printed circuit boards, fiber optics, etc. And these are the only ones we know about.

Just in the fields of aviation and aerospace, remarkable advances were

---

[73] https://en.wikipedia.org/wiki/Aluminium_oxynitride
[74] https://www.amazon.com/UFO-Secrets-Inside-Wright-Patterson-Eyewitness/dp/1938875184

made in the '50s and '60s. Aircraft went from subsonic speeds (approx. 700mph) to Mach 6.7 (4,560mph) with the development of the X-15 experimental rocket-powered aircraft[75] and Mach +3 (2,200mph) for the USAF operational SR-71 jet aircraft[76].

These were in the '60s. Imagine what craft exists today. R&D hasn't stood still. It's just we don't know what's out there now. It's thought that ET technology has been integrated into *dark* aerospace research and space programs. Thus, what better source to gain a glimpse of what this technology entails?

A Technology "Heads Up"

One of the leading companies in this research has been Lockheed Martin.[77] The following are very revealing comments made by Ben Rich[78], the former head of their Advanced Development Company (commonly known as the Skunkworks division) from 1975 to 1991, who is quoted as having made the following statements, both during presentations and in conversations with individuals.

"We already have the means to travel around the stars, but these technologies are locked up in black projects, and it would take an act of God to ever get them out to benefit humanity." (source: a statement made after UCLA presentation to three Disclosure Project[79] witnesses)

"We now have the technology to take ET back home." (source: UCLA School of Engineering Alumni speech 3/23/93)

---

[75] https://en.wikipedia.org/wiki/North_American_X-15
[76] https://en.wikipedia.org/wiki/Lockheed_SR-71_Blackbird
[77] https://www.lockheedmartin.com/en-us/index.html
[78] https://www.lockheedmartin.com/en-us/news/features/history/rich.html
[79] https://en.wikipedia.org/wiki/Steven_M._Greer

"There is an error in the equations, and we have figured it out, and now know how to travel to the stars, and it won't take a lifetime to do it." (source: UCLA School of Engineering Alumni speech 3/23/93)

"It is time to end all secrecy on this, as it no longer poses a national security threat, and make the technology available for use in the private sector." (source: UCLA School of Engineering Alumni speech 3/23/93)

"There are many in the intelligence community who would like to see this stay in the black and not see the light of day." (source: UCLA School of Engineering Alumni speech 3/23/93)

"The Air Force has just given us a contract to take ET back home." (source: 1993 WPAFB slide presentation)

"Jim, we have things out in the desert that are fifty (50) years beyond what you could possibly comprehend. If you have seen it on Star Wars or Star Trek, we've been there, done that, or decided it was not worth the effort." (Source: direct comments by Ben Rich to Jim Goodall[80] via telephone call at the USC medical center approximately one week before Ben passed away on January 5th, 1995)

"Dear John, Yes, I'm a believer in both categories. Feel anything is possible. Many of our man-made UFOs were unfunded opportunities. In both categories, there are a lot of books and charlatans; be careful. Best regards, Ben Rich." (source: 7/21/86 letter to John Andrews (Testors model Corporation) from Ben Rich who asked Ben if he was a believer in A) man-made UFOs, and B) extra-terrestrial UFOs)

"We have some new things. We are not stagnating. What we are doing is updating ourselves without advertising. There are some new programs, and there are certain things- some of them 20 or 30 years old- that are still break-throughs and appropriate to keep quiet about. Other people don't have them yet. (source: statement made by Ben Rich to Stuart F. Brown in

---

[80] https://podtail.com/en/podcast/exploring-unexplained-phenomena/2-16-19-jim-goodall-aviation-and-science-writer/

an interview published in Popular Science October 1994[81])

"I wish I could tell you about the projects we are currently working on. They are both fascinating and fantastic. They call for technologies once only dreamed of by science fiction writers." (source: AIAA lecture Atlanta, Ga. September 7-9 1988)

Rebuttal

As a point of reference, I'm including a link below[82] to comments made by Steve Justice[83] , who worked with Mr. Rich at Lockheed Martin. This reference contains his response to a question about the earlier quotation: *"We now have the technology to take ET back home."*

In it, he characterizes Mr. Rich's statement as a joke. His suggestion that he may have had a strong sense of humor is quite likely, but there's no sense of this in these statements. Additionally, I doubt this would be a consistent theme when he's making presentations to his engineering peers. Added to this is the number of times he made similar or substantiating statements to others. I understand Mr. Justice's job is naturally to *explain away* these controversial quotes, but his effort here is not at all convincing – particularly given the level and history of this topic's secrecy. And, of particular note, no denial was made of what Mr. Rich stated.

These statements, combined with what is observed with the UFO phenomenon, suggest capabilities that redefine conventional science as we know it today. First, the ability of ETs to travel to Earth suggests an ability to transcend the Galaxy. This either invalidates our knowledge of the speed of light being a limit to space travel or suggests an ability to somehow bypass this limit. Either or both redefine our science.

And what's really enlightening is Mr. Rich's statements were made over 30

---

[81]https://books.google.com/books?id=VWYCwRFRpJUC&printsec=frontcover&source=gbs_ge_summary_r&cad=0#v=onepage&q&f=false

[82] https://www.instagram.com/p/CDkZ_QbhsKd/?hl=en

[83] https://investors.virgingalactic.com/governance/board-of-directors/person-details/default.aspx?ItemId=d36ddc89-1ccb-4232-b2dc-1a536f982dab

years ago. Imagine the progress since then.

So, Where's the Evidence?
Combining this with all the other information available only confirms what Mr. Rich says. One of the most convincing sources mentioned was Mr. William Mills Tompkins, who had experience in the U.S. Navy and several subsequent aerospace

contractors. It all adds up to very convincing evidence of secret space programs that have been in existence for decades.

Actually, it's almost everywhere in the UFO literature. One of the most common speculations in recent years is that many UFO sightings are actually of Earth origin, coming from gained ET technology. An often-cited example is the TR-3B spacecraft[84]. Evidence of this triangular craft comes from many independent sources. Experiencers even include military personnel (whistleblowers) who've actually flown on them during their missions. Several of Michael E. Salla's more recent books are excellent sources for more detail with these.

The Energy Connection
Another remarkable capability associated with UFOs is their energy source. Here's a quote from Harold E. Puthoff, M. S. E., Ph.D., a 38-year-old specialist in quantum physics, parapsychology, and paraphysical phenomena[85].

"So-called empty space isn't really empty at all. It's actually full of energy."[86]

This is a fairly constant theme in the books on UFOs concerning their energy source. Think of the consequences and value of this technology. It has the potential to make any country energy-independent. It also has tremendous

---

[84] https://en.wikipedia.org/wiki/Black_triangle_(UFO)
[85] https://www.cia.gov/readingroom/document/cia-rdp96-00787r000100220005-4
[86] https://www.amazon.com/Unacknowledged-Expose-Worlds-Greatest-Secret/dp/1943957045

military value. This isn't to mention the resultant benefits to the environmental and climate issues Earth is now facing. (This will be examined further in the economics chapter.)

Paranormal Phenomena – Telepathy and Manipulating Time
Another of the most common unexplained mysteries encountered is telepathy – communication without voice. This is almost universally reported with ETs. It's their ability to understand our thoughts and, for many experiencers, to understand the ETs' thoughts *in their minds.* But, this is only one phenomenon that is outside of current science's ability to explain.

Others include startling and unbelievable reports concerning the manipulation of time. And yet, there are numerous credible accounts of this. There are witnesses who've seen the ability to look into the future and alter current directions based on the outcome. There are also individuals reporting being recruited to experience years of life, only to return to the present – not having aged. Typically, these individuals have no memory of this occurring, with their minds being erased of any recall. But, isolated examples have occurred where people have retained their memory. Some of these include the following examples.

A True Account of One Man's Twenty-Year Abduction
The experience described by Tony Rodrigues' in his book *Ceres Colony Cavalier* initially defies belief. If it wasn't for the consistencies with numerous other sources, the obvious honesty in his account, the character reference of Dr. Salla, and the consistency of the details provided, one would be tempted to attribute it to fiction. But, like a number of other reveals related to the UFO/ET phenomenon, it's, in all probability, unfortunately true. I realize some are going to respond in disbelief to this, but think of this as just one contributing piece of evidence to a much larger puzzle. If you choose to read this source, its credibility will become more evident. And, as in one more reminder, believing this is not necessary since it's not the goal.

Mr. Rodrigues, as a 9-year-old child, had a *close encounter* at home in bed and was asked by a Reptilian alien: "Do you want to help us?"[87] He answered, "Of course" (as many would at that age). This led to a 20-year *career* as a slave. Equally remarkable is that he woke up the next morning after this experience as if nothing had happened. And, what's most remarkable is not that he was abducted or experienced this phenomenon, but that he remembered it.

In Tony Rodrigues' experience, this was a most gruesome, punishing experience – not for the faint of heart. His account of initially being employed as a drug-induced psychic child in Peru, then a sex slave in the Seattle area, a conscripted soldier on Mars fighting insectoid ETs, and finally as a slave crew member of a space-going freighter provides insights into the economic trade goods of the Draconian-German alliance. Normally, these abducted slaves have their memories *wiped*, but Mr. Rodrigues *fell through the cracks* and was able to avoid this. Incidentally, in both the sexual and crew-member roles, his superiors spoke German. This leads to important clues to the contents of the following chapters on recent history.

Another 20 and Back Experiencer
In his book *Twenty And Back,* Will Beaudoin describes his involvement in a similar program as a member of the Canadian Armed Forces (CAF).[88] It is revealed that as a child, he was recruited into an ET program that imparted wisdom and knowledge beyond his years. During this program, he travelled underground across North America. On one of these, he was tasked to escort some children he recognized from his off-duty time while in the CAF in Canada. On this particular occasion, he was to transport several indigenous children on underground trains to Dulce, New Mexico. During this mission, he asked the officer receiving them about their welfare. He received a blank stare and was later confronted by this with his commanding officer. These extracurricular duties were part of his twenty-and-back service in an undisclosed space program.

---

[87] Tony Rodrigues, *CERES COLONY CAVALIER*, 1st Ed. (Las Vegas, self-published, 2022), page 28, https://www.tonyrodrigues.com
[88] https://www.amazon.com/Twenty-Back-Will-Beaudoin-ebook/dp/B08WCHN8DV

Still Another Example

On January 31, 2022, in an interview with Dr. Michael E. Salla on *Exopolitics Today*[89], another twenty-and-back witness, David Rousseau, discusses his extraterrestrial experiences, service in the US-French secret space program, covert missions to Mars, and knowledge of different extraterrestrial organizations interacting with humanity. David's public emergence, along with the testimony of Jean Charles Moyen, provides important eyewitness accounts of the existence of a joint US-French secret space program and its evolution into an international secret space program.

At age eight, David Rousseau was recruited into a secret space program jointly run by the US and France and served for 20 years before being age-regressed and returned back in time to 1981. In this first interview for an English-speaking audience, David explains how an alien abduction at age six first brought him to the attention of secret space program authorities. He was recognized to have exceptional psychic and intuitive abilities, which led to him accepting an offer from an American general (who spoke French) to join a joint secret space program. In 1981, David was sent to Area 51 for his initial training and induction into a joint secret space program called Solar Warden. He was then sent to serve on the Solaris, one of at least two large spacecraft belonging to the US-French Secret Space Program. There, he met with Maria Orsic, who trained him and other children to develop their psychic abilities. It was during his initial service on the Solaris that David met Jean Charles Moyen (another US-French secret space program participant), who was then aged 12, and they became firm friends and colleagues. Their mutual recognition 40 years later is discussed in the second volume of David's four-volume series of books, which was recently published in French and will soon be available in English.

It's worthy to note the references to the Solar Warden USN program and Maria Orsic – both having been introduced previously by William Mills Tompkins in his book *Selected By Extraterrestrials.)*

---

[89] https://podtail.com/en/podcast/exopolitics-today-with-dr-michael-salla/2nd-french-secret-space-program-20-back-witness-em/

Influence by Combining Technology & the Paranormal

By combining the technology and the paranormal elements, there's evidence suggesting the ability to influence societies as described in the previous chapter. It's obvious the value this would have on persuading the population to adopt favorable policies and selection of sympathetic leaders to the aliens' objectives. As stated previously, there's circumstantial evidence that this has occurred repeatedly in recent history...and is occurring now in the U.S.

The threat to the planet of this type of influence is particularly of concern. Any government opposed to being exploited by covert colonization would make this a top priority. This is an existential threat and *a need to know.*

Putting It into Perspective

With this brief introduction to the technology and paranormal abilities evidenced by UFOs and ETs, one can begin to appreciate the potential value these elements have to any government. It's obvious what the previously hinted at technology and paranormal abilities might offer any society. History has proven those possessing the most technology always have an enormous advantage. As a result, technology offers opportunities that are difficult to overvalue. When it comes to UFOs and ETs, the technology demonstrated redefines reality. Once you begin to study this topic, you soon realize that the subject extends far beyond questions just concerning UFO and ET's existence.

For governments and military leaders, the real focus is on the technology and its implications. This is an obvious reason for the secrecy. And this marks the transition in how UFOs/ETs influence our society indirectly in covert ways. And, with this transition, you'll learn this is where the real questions and answers are found – with matters related to energy, politics, national security, and recent history.

UNBELIEVABLE

CHAPTER 11 THE ECONOMICS

Follow the Money
In our society, this is the motto that frequently leads to a lot of answers. It's no different from extraterrestrials (ETs) interactions with humans on Earth. As physical life forms, we value assets that promote survival. We've already outlined the motives involving the exploitation of the Earth's resources. These not only include minerals but also human and animal wealth. DNA appears to be a cherished commodity among aliens, given the countless experiencers being abducted to harvest DNA, human hybridization programs, and related animal mutilations. These, and the evidence of dark government involvement, suggest the value of these as trade items. Slavery, psychic exploitation, and even humans and animals as food goods are mentioned as commercial products as well, with some aliens.

With this in mind, the following example illustrates these concerns.

2009 Indonesian UFO Abductions
A striking *Lehto Files* YouTube video has been produced by author and well-known producer Chris Lehto, where he interviews a U.S. Marine veteran, Michael Herrera.[90] Chris Lehto is a retired USAF F-16 pilot with both Bachelor's and Master's degrees in science.[91] He is also a respected UFO/ET researcher.

Herrera came forward recently to publicly relate an experience he had 14 years earlier, as a Marine supporting humanitarian relief mission.[92] This occurred in Indonesia following the 2009

[90] https://www.youtube.com/watch?v=nTu8UZuDugc
[91] https://us.amazon.com/stores/author/Chris Lehto
[92] https://www.dailymail.co.uk/news/article-12177943

Sumatra earthquake, resulting in a tsunami in the region.[93] In April 2023, he testified under oath to the government's UFO investigation team, the All-domain Anomaly Resolution Office (AARO), and a U.S. Senate committee. This is one former soldier being enabled by the recent Congressional legislation protecting whistleblowers in cases like this.

He was part of a mission guarding an airdrop of aid supplies outside the city of Padang in October of that year. This was in response to concerns regarding potential resistance or interference from local terrorists. In this capacity, his six-man unit stumbled across a hovering octagonal UFO he estimated as about a football field in diameter (300ft). It was supported by a clandestine U.S. military force. When Herrera's unit encountered this covert operation, they were disarmed and threatened at gunpoint by eight men. They all wore all-black camouflage uniforms and bullet-proof vests and wielded M4 rifles with high-end night vision attachments given to elite US troops. They were clearly an elite covert dark U.S. unit protecting the UFO mission.

Without going into detail (which are in the reference below), they were warned they would go to prison and potentially die if they talked to anyone about this incident. Because they returned early from their mission, they were interviewed several times – not disclosing what occurred. When their ship docked in the Philippines, he had his camera's memory card and battery stolen from a locked locker. All of their phones were taken as well. Returning to Japan, they were interviewed again and reminded of the consequences if they had ever talked to anyone about this incident.

Yet Another Incident Revealing a Disturbing Truth
The most disturbing realization coming from this was the evidence of this encounter involving human trafficking. This further supports a multitude of similar witnesses suggesting the CIA has worked collaboratively with aliens to kidnap people. In this case, it's apparent that these dark forces and their alien partners leverage disasters such as this to mask their abduction agenda, by attributing these lost souls to the disaster itself. In this case, Herrera's team witnessed military vehicles unloading containers suspected

---

[93] https://www.google.com/search?q=2009+sumatra+earthquake

of containing people onto the UFO loading platform.

For anyone unfamiliar with this – particularly for those serving our nation – it's difficult to express their shock and disappointment to find yourself associated with this type of activity. As evidenced by numerous other eyewitness accounts, there appears to be often a link between dark elements in the government and aliens that are exploiting humans in the worst possible imaginable ways.

I realize how the exploitation human and animal resources are both troubling and probably hard to believe, but again, there's ample evidence in the vast UFO/ET information available. This is another example where the multitude of experiences (in the thousands probably) support this. It's not just the numbers, but the diverse sources and common experiences. If you read Ardy Sixkiller Clarke's books[94], this becomes evident. Virtually all of the sources report commonalities that can't be shrugged off as mere coincidences. Preston Dennett[95] is another great source. As well as Dr. Michael E. Salla's extensive books[96], Steven M. Greer M.D.[97], and many, many more.

Earth's Opportunities

With the previous chapter's examination of the technology, we now understand the value of this to governments, including national security and associated political and economic dominance. This is only part of the equation, though. With the hidden business interests, there are great trade opportunities as well. Earth's manufactured goods, as it turns out, are a valuable commodity to ETs. Combined, these all encourage governments, businesses, and exploitive aliens to work together for mutual benefit. As you've now learned, there are a lot of reasons for this to occur, and it suggests they work together quietly already. The existence of ETs only further supports this mutually beneficial – but unfortunate for the rest of us – relationship.

---

[94] https://www.amazon.com/stores/Ardy-Sixkiller-Clarke/author/B00AQGBE9O
[95] https://www.amazon.com/stores/Preston-E.-Dennett/author/B0034PEPRCe
[96] https://www.amazon.com/stores/Michael-E.-Salla/author/B001HQ3F6C
[97] https://www.amazon.com/stores/Steven-M.-Greer/author/B00J23GXO8

Summary

There are countless sources of evidence supporting the economic relations defined here. If you've read any of the previously quoted sources, you've encountered much of it already. This chapter basically outlines the economics coming from the technology and the other stakeholders' objectives. This *sets the stage* for the following chapters in describing what has occurred in recent history and how this presents a *need to know* to any reader.

UNBELIEVABLE

CHAPTER 12 THE POLITICS

If you're like me, the last thing on my mind, when I started studying Unidentified Flying Objects (UFOs) and Extraterrestrials (ETs) was politics. But, as you might suspect at this point, it soon became a dominant focus – principally as a result of the secrecy. You simply can't learn anything about this topic without confronting all the associated efforts by the government to instill doubt, denial, cover-up, deception, trivialization, and ridicule with anything involving this topic.

Digging deeper, you soon realize concerns about the government go much farther than just the secrecy. The information available reveals truths that are inescapable and shocking since they reveal portions of the U.S. Government that are outside the Constitutional authority of what we know as our government. It exposes the reality of a *dark government* that's composed of a covert wealthy elite, a military-industrial complex, elite scientists, and other unknown entities. The more you learn, this is an increasingly inescapable realization. It not only pervades virtually everything about this topic but defines the context of UFOs/ETs as well.

This leads to the inevitable question of why. If you haven't noticed, the previous chapters have been a progression of questions leading up to answering the ultimate question and the subject of Chapter 19, *The Real Reasons For The Secrecy.* Surprisingly, though, this is only one of the key questions that has remained essentially unanswered. There are other less obvious ones as well, which you'll soon learn. Answering these is one the principal goals of this text. With all of this in mind, it's useful to review some of the basics involving governments in general.

Background

Merriam-Webster defines *government* as the following.[98]

Government –

1) the body of persons that constitutes the governing authority of a political unit or organization,
2) such a group in a parliamentary system constituted by the cabinet or by the ministry,
3) the act or process of governing,
4) the continuous exercise of authority over and the performance of functions for a political unit,
5) political science - studied economics and government, and
6) the office, authority, or function of governing.

With this, it's useful to focus on the objectives of a governing body. In general, there are four main purposes of government: 1) to establish laws, 2) to maintain order and provide security, 3) to protect citizens from external threats, and 4) to promote the general welfare by providing public services.[99]

Now, let's examine this relative to the topic of UFOs and ETs. Some immediate points of interest arise from these. First, maintain order and provide security. Second, protection of citizens from external threats. And finally, promoting the general welfare. Each of these is directly concerned with the UFO/ET phenomenon. With public welfare, you'll learn in Chapter 19 the specific substantial concerns with technology, energy, economic, and related political matters. Additionally, being unknown and external influences, UFOs and ETs raise issues of both security and potential threats.

UFO-Specific Concerns

Sightings of UFOs have posed concerns with both security and threats since the early '40s. During WWII, Allied personnel reported repeated incidents of encountering foo fighters, a term describing unknown objects observed

---

[98] https://www.merriam-webster.com/dictionary/government
[99] https://www.google.com/search?q=government+goals+and+objectives

by pilots. At the time, they were suspected to be evidence of advanced Nazi technology, despite the fact that there was no evidence that they ever posed a threat.

With the beginning of the Cold War, UFO sightings were often attributed to Soviet Union technology. This was heightened by frequent sightings around nuclear facilities. There were instances of UFOs deactivating nuclear missiles, which even amplified the fears of the Pentagon.[100]

Ever since the '40s, when both civilian and military encountered UFOs, anxieties have been raised about the potential for mid-air collisions. This has continued to today. This is a repeated theme in the reporting of UFO encounters. Initially, pilots were hesitant to report such incidents for fear of ridicule, notoriety, or reprisal. And these were well justified. Only in recent decades has this changed to a degree with the establishment of formal government reporting procedures.

But, where the real politics exist is with the hidden wealthy elites and their government agents. The following two examples provide a glimpse into this unseen world influence.

Unknown Elite Military
Several countries possess stealthy exclusive military special forces groups. For reference, there's an excellent April 17, 2017, *Business Insider* online article titled "The eight most elite special forces in the world."[101] These are soldiers who are trained to perform missions without any emotional, ethical, or moral concerns. They simply follow orders.

In their book *Planetary Intervention*, Ted Heidk (with the help of Fabio Santos) describes how Heidk was recruited into a covert international military that performed missions throughout the world.[102] Originally from Brazil, he was part of an elite force that intervened in multiple conflicts, as well as special operations against ETs. The book describes how an absence

---

[100] https://www.google.com/search?q=UFOs+deactivating+nuclear+missiles
[101] https://www.businessinsider.com/most-elite-special-forces-in-on-earth
[102] https://www.amazon.com/Planetary-Intervention-Fabio-Santos-ebook/dp/B07VX95T5J

of emotional considerations is a key element. On numerous occasions, innocent civilians were killed to accomplish the mission objectives.

Fabio Santos actually writes all but one of the chapters based on Heidk's experiences. The one written by Heidk himself is a sincere and deeply felt conviction expressing his opposition to the existence of these clandestine forces outside of any real authority. It's clear that he's writing this from experience and values. This book exposes hidden militaries that are directed by unknown sources. In the case of one, it's suspected to be an alliance with ETs.

With this in mind, the following is an yet another more extreme example of this type of military force without limits. It is both shocking, and one most people won't believe. This is despite the wealth of evidence and its clear viability. It's all about wealth and power.

The 2018 Hawaii Incident
At 8:08 AM on the morning of January 13, 2018, an alert was issued via the Emergency Alert System and Wireless Emergency Alert System over television, radio, and cellular networks in the U.S. state of Hawaii, instructing citizens to seek shelter due to an incoming ballistic missile.[103]

The message read:

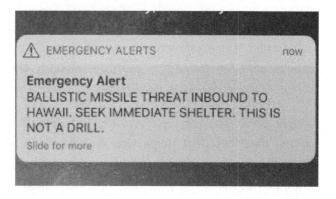

Thirty-eight minutes later, state officials blamed a miscommunication during a drill at the state's Hawaii Emergency Management Agency for the first message. David Ige, the governor, apologized for the erroneous alert.

---

[103]https://en.wikipedia.org/wiki/2018_Hawaii_false_missile_alert.

The Federal Communications Commission and the Hawaii House of Representatives launched investigations into the incident, leading to the resignation of the state's emergency management administrator.[104]

This occurred during a time of escalating tensions between the U.S. and N. Korea. It was all a result of increasingly volatile rhetoric between the two leaders, President Donald Trump and Kim Jong Un. In response to this, N. Korea was increasing testing of offensive ballistic missiles to the point where it was suspected they had the capability of striking Hawaii with a nuclear weapon.

On the surface, this all makes sense. Unfortunately, there's additional evidence putting this explanation in severe question, with considerable concerns.

First, television broadcasts by both NBC (KHNL) and CBS (KGMB) in Hawaii were interrupted by an emergency message stating the missile alert was from the U.S. Pacific Command (PACOM), not the State of Hawaii. (Note the discrepancy in the source of the emergency notification.)

Second, there were numerous eyewitnesses to the Pearl Harbor Naval Station activating its emergency sirens and evacuating personnel. This was later confirmed by military personnel. This contradicts the Hawaii investigation, which found that PACOM did not issue the alert and that it only came from the state's emergency agency.

Third, more eyewitnesses observed an object exploding high over the Hawaiian Islands about the time of the alert. One of these was a boat tour group. Reported to have occurred at 8:00am, this was substantiated by them being interviewed on the local news, which was shortly after pulled. The sightings and local news reports were confirmed by numerous individuals throughout the region. Later, local residents reported they were visited and intimidated by police and other authorities to remain silent. Later, a Maui boat captain said he'd never seen so many U.S. Coast Guard ships in the area – possibly searching for debris.

---

[104] *US Air Force Secret Space Programs*, Michael E. Salla, PH.D., pages 377-396.

I could go on, but the information available suggests this was an attempted *false flag attack*. Meaning that someone staged this attack to achieve their own ends, at another's expense – in this case falsely blaming N. Korea. In other words, an unknown assailant wanted to start a war by making it appear to come from N. Korea. Fortunately, cooler heads at the White House recognized it as such and did not retaliate.

Note the history relative to this plan. It's not the first attack on Hawaii to start a war. That's what prompted the U.S. to enter WWII. There's firm precedence for someone to think that it would be successful, particularly with the state of relations between the two nations and their leaders at the time.

Just to add credence to this chain of events, sources on the internet with supposed close ties to the military and Administration posted information predicting a DEVCON 1 event (signifying nuclear war is imminent) six days prior to January 13th.

If one *buys into the theory* that a missile was intercepted, it's interesting to consider who might have this capability and would have accomplished it. Five months earlier, following a failed attempt the previous year, the U.S. Navy was able to intercept a medium-range ballistic missile over the Pacific. And yet, another test on January 30th was a second failure. This suggests that it did not have a reliable ability to intercept incoming missile threats. It also turns out that the USAF operates advanced space tracking systems in Hawaii. These may have been involved in the shoot-down. This, along with the sightings of numerous UFOs following the incident, suggests either a secret capability of a USAF Space Program, possibly in collaboration with beneficial ETs.

In response to questions about how this could occur, one source claimed CIA operatives took control of a USN nuclear missile submarine that had been the source of the attack.[105] This is suspect at best, but information suggests it may have some truth.

---

[105] *US Air Force Secret Space Programs*, Michael E. Salla, PH.D., page 396.

THE POLITICS

Summary

The politics with UFOs and ETs becomes apparent as one digs deeper into the subject matter. One soon realizes that both the crimes against humanity and the corruption undermine the democratic principles that U.S. citizens believe we live under with the protections provided by the Constitution. Like the UFO/ET phenomenon as a whole, things are not like they appear. Another *need to know* for everyone.

PART IV HISTORY – WHERE IT'S ALL AT

CHAPTER 13 PRE-MODERN HISTORY

Evidence of Unidentified Flying Objects (UFOs) and Extraterrestrials (ETs) is as old as the earliest human tales, writings, and recorded history.

Inexplainable Evidence from Antiquity
In addition to the referenced sources in Chapter 5 from antiquity, there's also curious evidence of ETs from documentation in the form of prehistoric art. The following are only a small number of examples. These are from cultures throughout the world.

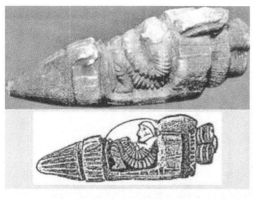

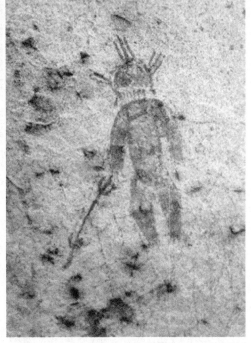

While none of these images offer proof of extraterrestrial contact in the past, they do prompt the question: where did the inspiration for these come from? Why is this type of evidence consistently found throughout the world? And, why do indigenous peoples universally believe in the existence of UFOs and ETs?

This goes without mentioning all the archeological ruins – many of which remain unexplained as to how or why they were constructed.

Further supporting this is a list of reported UFO sightings online at Wikipedia that have occurred in recorded history. While this is only a partial listing, it does reflect the fact that they have consistently been observed over this period of time.[106]

---

[106] https://en.wikipedia.org/wiki/List_of_reported_UFO_sightings#By_location

CHAPTER 14 PRE-WWII GERMANY

What's sad about the topic of Unidentified Flying Objects (UFOs) and Extraterrestrials (ETs) is you can't go to a museum and see a Nazi Haunebu UFO or even meet or converse with an ET. The people who come forward with personal experience are few and far between. This is particularly true of pre-WWII Nazi Germany. One reason is that almost everyone from that period has now died from old age. The other reason is extreme secrecy.

As an example of this, there's evidence that during the closing phases of WWII, the Nazi's SS closed an underground plant at Kahla, Germany, and sent all the slave labor to Buchenwald to be killed in the gas chambers.[107] All the German scientists and staff were relocated to South America or other points south.

Sources of Information
As a result of the secrecy, the missing personnel, and the fact that this all occurred about 100 years or so ago only adds to the scarcity of information about what transpired at the beginning of the Nineteenth century in Germany. What little that is known comes from hearsay from whistleblowers like William Mills Tompkins and others. Some come from German and other eastern Europeans, as well as U.S. Naval (USN) intelligence personnel, who were apparently deeply embedded in the Nazi regime. And there are numerous personal accounts from obscure witnesses and others that are beyond the scope of this text to detail here.

One I couldn't help but mention, though, is an interesting report regarding a mission on March 13, 1917, during WWI. Baron Manfred Von Richthofen, known as the German military aviator the Red Baron, shortly after sunrise accompanied by his wingman Peter Waitzrik. Their dawn patrol was suddenly interrupted by a large metallic disk flying directly in front of them. It was roughly 140ft in diameter. The Baron immediately opened fire, and the craft went into some trees. Two "little baldheaded guys" were seen

---

[107] Michael E. Salla, Ph.D., *Exopolitics – Political Implications of the Extraterrestrial Presence*, Tempe, Dandelion Books Publication, 2004, page 121.

climbing out and running away.[108] Following this encounter, they were both told never to mention it again. Waitzrik later spent his career as a Lufthansa flight captain – a reputable source. The question with this is not whether it was a UFO with ETs, but whether it was an ET ally of Germany at the time.

The German-Alien Alliances
What is known is that Germany then possessed a strong psychic culture that spawned channeling communications with ETs. This was at a time when the U.S., the Soviet Union, and other European countries were averse to this paranormal phenomenon. Times changed, though, as both the U.S. and Soviet Union later learned of Germany's success in this field of study, and subsequently aggressively adopted these methodologies.

As described previously in Chapter 5, there's considerable evidence of Nazi Germany possessing ET technology prior to World War Two (WWII). The U.S. Navy's intelligence network reported two concurrent ongoing UFO programs at the time in Germany. The one by the SS, but another one led by Maria Orsitsch[109], also known as Maria Orsic. As mentioned previously, a famous German medium who later became the leader of the Vril Society. According to the agent, when she was 16 in 1911, she was instructed by ETs to construct a large spaceship and move her and her family to a planet in another star system.

By 1934, this effort had produced an advanced ET-based technology craft that utilized anti-gravity. At the same time, another German occult group, the Thule Society similarly, was working with another ET group – this one being an ancient Earth civilization populating subterranean regions on the poles and other locations.[110] Hitler's support for these efforts was evidenced by the SS taking over and strongly staffing the research into these

---

[108] Frank Joseph, *Military Encounters with Extraterrestrials*, Rochester, Bear & Company, 2018, page 14.
[109] https://www.amazon.com/Maria-orsic-originated-created-earths/dp/1300599375/ref=sr_1_1?crid=2HZBPAGD4DII&keywords=maria+orsic+book&qid=1698609489&sprefix=maria+orsic+%2Caps%2C115&sr=8-1
[110] Salla, *Exopolitics*, pg. 112.

projects involving ET technologies.[111]

Supporting this, as reported in the July 6, 2023 issue of *Popular Mechanics*, an article by Sascha Brodsky titled "A Researcher Says the First UFO Really Crashed in Italy in 1933. And He Has Evidence. – Secret documents suggest a suspicious cover-up."[112] What's interesting about this is it has ties to a current whistleblower, former U.S. intelligence officer David Grusch. In all probability, the craft crashed and recovered was a Nazi UFO. It also states that at the end of WWII, the U.S. confiscated the remains, which is entirely consistent with other similar reports of the period (and since).

Herman Oberth, the famous former Nazi German scientist and the father of modern rocketry, is shown here in the foreground of the photo with other U.S. Army Ballistic Missile Agency (ABMA) scientists (including Dr. Wernher von Braun). When asked where the advanced technology Germany possessed came from, he said they "we cannot take credit," they "have been helped" by "peoples of other worlds."[113]

The image to the right is of a commercial 1/72 scale plastic model (produced by Squadron[114]) of the Haunebu II, a suspected Nazi UFO developed during the latter stages of WWII. This is illustrative of the technology being developed by Nazi Germany leading up to the Second World War. Obviously, this isn't evidence, but it

---

[111] Salla, *Exopolitics*, pg. 112.
[112]
https://www.popularmechanics.com/military/research/a44466099/researcher-says-he-has-evidence-of-1933-ufo-crash-in-italy/
[113] Salla, *Exopolitics*, pg. 115.
[114] https://www.squadron.com

does collaborate with other independent sources, and illustrate the level of detail provided by various sources of the Nazi UFO technology. These aren't people's imagination.

Associated Nazi Germany Expeditions
Coincident with the German alliance in developing advanced ET technologies, was a similar exploration and research in various regions throughout the globe. It appears that these were aimed at two ends. One is to establish bases in remote regions. And two, to recover ET artifacts and technology. It's reported that an operational craft was recovered by this means, further suggesting that they were assisted in this by ETs.[115]

This apparently also led to several expeditions to the South Pole region. The first occurred in 1901-03, producing 20 volumes of reports and two atlases outlining the findings – the last being published in 1931. The second exploration was in 1911-13. However, the most revealing was the third in 1938-39. Ostensibly for the purpose of establishing a whaling base, Germany launched an expedition arriving off of Dronning Maud Land on January 19, 1939, and began charting the region and planting Nazi flags. Two aircraft also took over 16,000 aerial photos of the region, encompassing more than hundreds of thousands of square kilometers. On its return, the expedition made stops along the coast of Brazil, returning to Hamburg on April 11, 1939.[116]

Controversy
The attention given to Antarctica suggests Germany's strong interest in this region during the first part of the twentieth century. One could attribute this to territorial ambitions, along with scientific and resource interests. The evidence of ET-related activities and interests certainly challenges one's senses. In fact, numerous sources, such as Wikipedia, consistently suggest that these are hoaxes and conspiracy theories. Another notable one is online in the form of an article titled "Hitler's Frozen Base" by *Cool*

---

[115] Salla, *Exopolitics*, pg. 110.
[116] https://frammuseum.no/shop/product/the-third-reich-in-antarctica-the-german-antarctic-expedition-1938-39/

Antarctica.[117] Both appear to be well presented and represent a rational view of the apparent ridiculousness of what is being presented.

It's difficult to know the truth in cases such as this. On the one hand, you have what appears to be normal, well-founded information that counters all the evidence suggesting otherwise. I have to admit that typically, I'd be siding with the nay-sayers. But here, there's just too much evidence suggesting otherwise. We have credible witnesses and informed leaders who make statements that clearly suggest there's truth behind the conspiracy theories. In my case, the ultimate findings are entirely consistent with the history that has been played out since then. This all will be revealed in subsequent chapters.

---

[117] https://www.coolantarctica.com/Community/antarctic-mysteries-hitlers-secret-base.php

CHAPTER 15 WWII GERMANY

As you know, the United States entered WWII with Japan's bombing of Pearl Harbor on December 7, 1941. As you might guess, this put the U.S. on notice of it being attacked by both Japanese and German forces on both coasts. While there are isolated cases of this occurring, one of the most notable did not appear to be an attack, and in all probability, did not relate to Axis sources.

The Battle of Los Angeles[118]
This occurred on the evening of 24 February 1942 into early morning the following day in southern California. As witnessed by William Mills Tompkins[119] (as you've learned about him in earlier chapters), while living in Long Beach, California at this time, he, his brother, and father (who was an officer in the Navy at that time) watched a series of UFOs from 8 pm through 3:30 am. What transpired that evening was coastal anti-

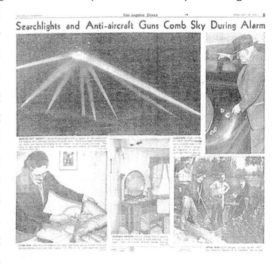

Searchlights and Anti-aircraft Guns Comb Sky During Alarm

aircraft batteries attempting to shoot down these craft – firing over 1,400 rounds with no apparent effect. As you might suspect, thousands of people witnessed this, which was later claimed to be the result of a weather balloon and the paranoia at the time following the attack on Pearl Harbor by the Japanese on December 7th, 1941. Later, Tompkins heard that two of the smaller UFOs had been shot down and recovered.

Foo Fighters and Related Reports
Throughout the war, Allied aircrews reported encountering numerous

---

[118] https://en.wikipedia.org/wiki/Battle_of_Los_Angeles
[119] https://www.amazon.com/Selected-Extraterrestrials-secret-think-tanks-secretaries-ebook/dp/B01IK2N38U?ref_=ast_author_mpb

unidentified aerial phenomena. I use this descriptor since they often don't conform to the more typical disc-shaped UFO types. However, they did exhibit similar behavior with excessive speeds, exceptional maneuverability, and being impervious to conventional weapons. In fact, these encounters weren't limited to the Allies; German and Japanese pilots also reported these. What also was in common was the secrecy involved.

Nazi Germany

As outlined in the previous chapter, there's a great deal of obscure but credible evidence suggesting that Nazi Germany possessed Extraterrestrial (ET) technology and had created working Unidentified Flying Objects (UFOs). With the unfolding events of WWII, this is where history begins to get very interesting.

By this time, the Allies – particularly the U.S., Soviet Union, Great Britain, and France had begun to realize the reality of these new Nazi technologies. Their inherent doubts concerning the psychic sources with ETs were eroded by the continuing evidence of the advancements Germany had made earlier in the century. One example of this is the Nazis had jet engine technology at the beginning of the war. This was in addition to their rocket technology and UFOs.

If it hadn't been for Hitler making mistakes in unnecessarily delaying these technologies, the outcome of the war might have differed since much of it was the result of the Allies' war based on attrition, eventually gaining clear air superiority. This allowed them to choke off fuel supplies to Germany.

Haunebu

Wikipedia describes Haunebu as "Any of a class of flying saucers supposedly built by the Nazis."[120] It seems Wikipedia takes a very 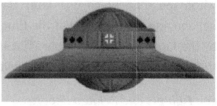 skeptical view of anything related to UFOs/ETs, let alone any history of Nazi Germany's development of UFOs and their interaction with ETs. In researching this period of Germany's ET technology, what's surprising is the

---

[120] https://en.wiktionary.org/wiki/Haunebu

overwhelming wealth of information about this UFO development. In particular, the consistency of the evidence regarding their development of the Haunebu. This includes documents of the designs and photos that surfaced in the late '80s and 1990s.[121] In addition to the reports of U.S. Naval agents leading up to WWII, there are multiple eyewitness instances during the war. These include Allied agents and local workers in the region. Adding to this are FBI and CIA documents following the war.[122] These UFOs were observed in locations other than Germany. This, and as you'll learn, similar reports after WWII throughout the globe with craft that have this same appearance. This includes substantial sightings in the U.S. (as you'll learn in the next chapter).

The Haunebu description pertains specifically to one of two principal types of UFOs developed by Germany. Concurrently, the Vril Society developed another smaller craft. These are both further detailed in David Hatcher Childress's book *Haunebu – The Secret Files* for anyone interested. The following information comes from this source.

As identified previously, the Haunebu design was of SS military origin. There were three models of these. The smaller Haunebu I first flew in 1939. It had a crew of eight, was 25-meters in diameter, and was initially capable of 4,800 km/h (3,000 mph). Apparently, later versions were able to attain 17,000 km/hr, or over 10,000 mph.

The Haunebu II, with a crew of twenty personnel, was flown in 1944, and two prototypes were completed. It was reportedly capable of 21,000 km/h (13,000 mph). A still larger Haunebu III with a 71-meter diameter was crewed by 32 men and could reach 40,000 km/h, or 25,000 mph. It's reported that this had an endurance of 7-8 weeks and

---

[121] David Hatcher Childress, *Haunebu – The Secret Files*, Kempton, Adventures Unlimited Press, 2021, pg. 11-13.
[122] Ibid, 15-20.

made 19 test flights.

As a further interesting note, it's reported that Germany sent a crew to Mars in 1943; however, they didn't return. And there were visits to the moon as well.

Secret Nazi Bases
As with the evidence of the Haunebu UFOs, there's also evidence of Nazi Germany establishing secret bases throughout the world, including Antarctica, Greenland, Tibet, and others. At this time, the Nazi U-boat fleet was extensive, and operated throughout the world. This, combined with their aircraft, allowed them to establish and maintain these bases. Some of them, even after WWII ended, as you'll learn.

Neuschwabenland and South America
As with the existence of German UFOs at this time, the Nazi occupation of Antarctica remains in question, according to many sources. However, there's substantial supporting evidence of its existence during WWII from numerous sources. As suggested earlier, the Vril Society in Germany is actually supposed to have achieved communications with an advanced underground civilization in the early part of the twentieth century. From this, they were able to receive instructions on how to create UFO craft.[123] Eight versions of this are described in David Hatcher Childress's book *Haunebu – The Secret Files*. Interestingly, all of these, as well as the Haunebu, were capable of being armed.

Apparently, it became evident in 1942 to some leaders in Nazi Germany that the war would, in all probability, be lost – with both the entry of the United States and the difficulties that had been encountered with securing Great Britain. As a result, plans were put in motion to surreptitiously transfer key assets to South America and Antarctica to ensure their continued survival. This transpired over the remaining period of the conflict and included wealth, manufacturing, and associated personnel – particularly those involved with advanced ET technologies. It's reported

---

[123] Michael E. Salla, Ph.D., *Galactic Diplomacy – Getting to Yes with ET*, Kealakekua, Exopolitics Institute, 2013, pages 93-95.

that the Haunebu III was utilized to evacuate Vril Society members – many being in the SS – to secret sites outside of Germany. This, along with the extensive U-boat fleet, was involved in the migration of resources.

When the Allies – the U.S. and the Soviets – were advancing in Germany and the final bastions of the Third Reich, there was little left of any remnants of their advanced technology capabilities. And, what was, was unsurprisingly secreted away.

CHAPTER 16 POST-WWII TO TURN OF THE CENTURY

Turning Point
The decade following WWII marks a significant turning point. A number of relatively unrelated occurrences led to the Unidentified Flying Object (UFO) and Extraterrestrial (ET) phenomenon to rise to the surface – both in the U.S. Government and in the general population. Prior to this, this topic remained largely out of sight of the public. (The Battle of Los Angeles was a marked exception.) UFOs and ETs were solely in the domain of military and government secrecy. From 1947 on, though, a rash of sightings and experiences prompted – not only heightened awareness and interest – but began to reveal the veil of secrecy surrounding this matter. Adding to this, the U.S. Government made a number of covert policy decisions that set in motion where we are today. The first of these occurred right at the end of WWII and had enormous hidden implications.

The following summarizes both the critical policy decisions, the relatively unknown events that resulted from these, and some notable ones that have garnered national attention. The length of this chapter reflects the significance of these.

Operation Paperclip
From the intelligence gathered during the war, the U.S. and its allies realized the advanced technologies the Germans possessed. This, combined with the anticipated Cold War competition for their associated resources at the end of the war (with the U.S. and allies approaching from the west and the Soviets from the east), created a rush to capture these assets. This included scientists, equipment, and any UFOs that might remain in Germany. This was also true of capturing Nazi intelligence personnel at the same time.

As a result, over 16,000 people (scientists, personnel, and their families) were brought to the U.S. and incorporated into society, both in government and industry. This included members of the Nazi SS as well as their intelligence agents. On the surface, this made complete sense to secure their secrets. With the Cold War looming, it was simply a matter of national security to ensure that much of this technological expertise was retained and kept out of the hands of the Soviets. The ethical and moral concerns with incorporating the former Nazi SS were secondary to the need for the technology. Unfortunately, this approach would have severe consequences.

One of the immediate unintended results was the infiltration of our intelligence, military, and science communities with continuing members of the Nazi fraternity. What was overlooked was these personnel's continued allegiance with their hidden Nazi brethren in South America and the Antarctic. The reality was Nazi power was not eliminated with the end of WWII. This shocking realization will made evident shortly.

With the *recruited* former Nazis, the U.S. inadvertently embedded their agents within the U.S. intelligence services. This would prove to have devastating consequences. From this point forward, the Fourth Reich (the element continuing after the defeat of Nazi Germany's Third Reich in WWII) would have insider information about the U.S.'s most secret policies, plans, and operations. This becomes of particular importance in the subsequent years.

Operation Highjump
Less than a year after the formal surrender of Japan on September 2, 1945, the U.S. embarked on a mission involving a substantial Naval taskforce to the South Pole. Ostensibly labeled as a research mission, a fleet of Navy ships left on August 6, 1946, bound for Antarctica. The 888-foot-long flagship was the aircraft carrier USS *Philippine Sea*. This ship had a contingent of 19 aircraft, including six R4Ds, the Navy version of the Douglas twin-engined C-47 transport (a military version of the DC-3). This was combined by a Martin PBM Mariner and a half-dozen Sikorsky helicopters on accompanying ships. These were joined by two tanker ships, two supply ships, and two icebreakers. All these were escorted by two destroyers and the submarine USS *Sennet*. Task Force 68 consisted primarily of military forces with little scientific personnel or research equipment. Admiral Richard E. Byrd, Jr. was in overall command of the mission. Admiral Byrd

described the mission as "My expedition has a military character."[124] (An added note here is that Admiral Bird had also been invited and joined Nazi Germany's 1939 expedition.)

The armada landed at the Bay of Whales on January 15, 1947. Originally scheduled as a six to eight-month mission, the fleet left 40 days after arriving, the remaining force joining the rest of the fleet returning to South America for repairs. During this brief period, its aircraft logged 220 hours of flight time, over 22,700 miles, and took 70,000 photographs of an area equal to half of the U.S. While a few of these were released to the public, most still remain classified to this day.

Upon arriving in Chile for repairs, the sailors defied orders and shared their experiences. One of these was, surprisingly, Admiral Byrd himself. In an interview in the Wednesday, March 5, 1947, edition of the Chilean newspaper El Mercurio, it read in part as follows:[125]

> *"Admiral Richard E. Byrd warned today that the United States should adopt measures of protection against the possibility of an invasion of the country by hostile planes coming from the polar regions. The admiral explained that he was not trying to scare anyone, but the cruel reality is that in case of a new war, the United States could be attacked by planes flying over one or both poles. This statement was made as part of a recapitulation of his own polar experience in an exclusive interview with International News Service. Talking about the recently completed expedition, Byrd said that the most important result of his observations and discoveries is the potential effect that they have in relation to the security of the United States. The fantastic speed with which the world is shrinking – recalled the admiral – is one of the most important lessons learned during his recent Antarctic exploration. I have to warn my compatriots that the time had ended when we were able to take refuge in our isolation and rely on the certainty that the*

---

[124] Frank Joseph, *Military Encounters with Extraterrestrials*, Rochester, Bear & Company, 2018, pages 72-82.
[125] https://en.wikipedia.org/wiki/Operation_Highjump

distances, the oceans, and the poles were a guarantee of safety."

What's particularly notable here, is that his warning portends the Washington DC flyovers – suggesting the source of the sighting in the early '50s.

Following Admiral Byrd's return to Washington D.C., he was interrogated by U.S. Security Services officers and never publicly referred to the mission again – as it was marked classified. This ended any disclosure by the personnel involved with the threat of the associated severe penalties.

However, Soviet intelligence was able to uncover what actually happened during the mission. According to a Stalin-era report surprisingly unclassified and released after the collapse of the Soviet Union in 1991, Task Force 68 encountered numerous brief, but devastating skirmishes with UFOs over the several weeks after its landfall in the Bay of Whales. This reported that "dozens" of officers and personnel were killed or wounded.[126] This is extensively reviewed in the book *Military Encounters with Extraterrestrials: The Real War of the Worlds* by Frank Joseph.[127]

Another interesting piece of information is attributed to Admiral Byrd's personal diary account of a flight on February 19, 1947. In this, he recounts an inner-worldly experience where their aircraft is escorted by two disk-shaped craft with insignias resembling swastikas to a city in a lush green valley. They land and are met by Nordic-appearing men speaking Germanic accents. Three hours overdue, they return to their departure base. This experience was never disclosed, and it only surfaced in his personal diary, which was discovered at the Ohio State University's Byrd Polar Research Institute in a mislabeled box of Byrd's memorabilia in late 1995.

This, and the other evidence contained in Frank Joseph's and other books referenced at the end of this chapter, makes a very convincing argument that a contingent of Nazis continued to survive after the war, both in South

---

[126] Ibid, *Military Encounters,* 80.
[127] https://www.amazon.com/Military-Encounters-Extraterrestrials-Real-Worlds/dp/159143324X

America and Antarctica, as well as potentially in several other regions. And that this force was free to deploy its ET technology to deter any conventional armed force. Note this is in striking contrast to the Nazi military during WWII. And it's an indication of things to come in the next decade. This will be further evidenced by the subsequent events described herein.

Subsequent Events

Operation Highjump is only a foreshadowing of a series of events where UFOs and ETs really come to the forefront of the public's attention. 1946-47 were pivotal years. The following events triggered national attention. UFO sightings struck an interest in the general public. And, when you review these, you begin to understand why. Not only are they from reputable sources, but they clearly reveal questions about government involvement, where some begin to suspect a concerted effort to cover up, deny, trivialize, and discredit what would otherwise be reputable reports. As these continue to unfold, these questions are only amplified with similar changing and questionable explanations.

1947 Washington State Sighting

In the United States, this began with a well-publicized sighting on June 24, 1947, by Kenneth Arnold, an American aviator and businessman. Flying a private CallAir A-2 light aircraft, he reported seeing a formation of nine shiny objects flying near Mount Rainier, Washington. He  estimated their speed to be in excess of 1,200 mph. This received widespread national attention and resulted in the coining of the phrase *flying saucer* description of this type of UFO.

Mr. Arnold was an experienced pilot with 4,000 hours of flying time logged and a member of an Idaho search and rescue unit at the time.[128] In 1940, he started his own company in Boise, Idaho, which sold and installed fire suppression systems. His job involved traveling around the Pacific Northwest region. Arnold was born on March 29, 1915, in Sebeka,

---

[128] https://airandspace.si.edu/stories/editorial/1947-year-flying-saucer

Minnesota. He grew up in Scobey, Montana. Having been an Eagle Scout and all-state football player in high school, he subsequently attended the University of Minnesota from 1934 to 35.[129] Not someone who'd make a false report of an incident like this. In fact, his sighting prompted a lifetime inquiry into UFOs. And it resulted in a lot of unwanted attention and personal embarrassment.

1947 Roswell, New Mexico
Almost everyone has heard of this, involving the reported crash of a UFO on a remote ranch near Roswell, New Mexico. Apparently occurring in late June, it wasn't reported to the local sheriff until July 6th. This was then referred to Roswell Army Air Field (RAAF, now Walker Air Force Base). On July 8, RAAF public information officer Walter Haut issued a press release stating that the military had recovered a "flying disc" near Roswell.[130] This was retracted by the Army the following day.

What's really interesting is the subsequent chain of explanations of what occurred by the Army. At first, it was claimed to be the remains of a conventional weather balloon. Following rumors of ETs being recovered, the Army then stated there were anthropomorphic dummies on board. Further reports finally resulted in claims that Russian surgically altered children (made to look like ETs) were recovered. Given the extensive information available about this event, I'll let you decide the veracity of the latter explanation – particularly with the knowledge of the following.

Following the initial report, the Army assigned Major Jesse Marcel and Captain Sheridan Cavitt returned with the rancher to recover the remains, which resulted in a news release of recovered wreckage of a crashed UFO. Only, this story was retracted and totally denied the next day. Years later, in 1978, a now-retired Jesse Marcel revealed that the recovered craft actually had been a UFO suspected of ET origin. Note this is further supported by the account of retired Senior Master Sgt. Matilda O'Donnell MacElroy's account in Chapter 5.

---

[129] https://en.wikipedia.org/wiki/Kenneth_Arnold
[130] https://en.wikipedia.org/wiki/Roswell_incident

Establishment of Majestic-12

Known commonly as MJ-12, this committee was established by executive order of U.S. President Harry S. Truman. Consisting of a secret committee of high-ranking scientists, CIA, military, and business leaders, along with key government officials; it was formed in 1947 to facilitate the recovery and investigation of ET spacecraft. It is credibly suggested that this group evolved over the next decade to sequester and totally control all of the activities pertaining to UFOs and ETs. This included managing substantial dark budget funding and related covert commercial development and production activities. And, the extent of this came to exclude the involvement of U.S. Presidents during this time – citing they didn't have a need to know.

This become evident in the Eisenhower administration. When he was denied access to UFO/ET matters, he threatened to storm Area 51 with Army troops. This didn't happen. However, the exclusion of the Presidential involvement continued. It's credibly suggested that John F. Kennedy was assassinated by the CIA, at least partially related to his persistent efforts to gain access to UFO/ET information, and his subsequent initiative to share this with Soviet leader Nikita Khrushchev. There's even evidence linking his relationship at the time with Marylin Monroe, and her threats to disclose UFO/ET information he'd shared with her. This apparently led to her "suicide." This may stretch most people's believability, but there is substantial evidence that has emerged suggesting all of this is true. A close friend and confidant of Ms. Monroe, Dorothy Kilgallen, also died mysteriously several years later.

Presidents Jimmy Carter and Bill Clinton both shared strong interests in UFOs and ETs. But both, according to all reports, were unable to accomplish this and were deterred from further follow up. You can imagine the impact of realizing a former President was assassinated as a result of his efforts to uncover these secrets. It would certainly be a strong deterrent.

Another Unintended Consequence

Reading William Mills Tompkins' book *Selected by Extraterrestrials* reveals a surprising fact that only came to light in the U.S. Government in 2015. As stated earlier, he was recruited as a teenager early in WWII and – because of his talents – was inserted into the highest level of Naval secrecy, distributing information coming from Nazi Germany at that time. It turns out that during this period, the U.S. Navy's intelligence corps was separate and distinct from the Army's and the OSS (the predecessor of the current CIA). As a result, with the deployment of Operation Paperclip, the Navy realized the government had been compromised by the insertion of Nazi agents and scientists.

Thus, the Navy never shared its intelligence with other branches of the government. The critical importance of this will be revealed as the result of the following subsequent events.

The Coercion Begins

From 1947-1951, the USAF received 615 UFO reports. In 1952 alone, they registered over 717. In the news media, over a six-month period that year, over 16,000 items about UFOs were published in 150 newspapers. This unprecedented flood of UFO sightings was not an accident or coincidence. Increasingly, ETs tried to gain the U.S. Government's cooperation. It appears benevolent ETs were attempting to persuade the U.S. to ban nuclear weapons. At the same time, exploitive ETs were similarly attempting to coerce the government to authorize access to the human population for various purposes (abductions, DNA harvesting, hybridization programs, etc.). Of course, the extent of this was not disclosed to the government at the time.

To this end, this culminated in the July 1952 Washington D.C. flyovers. At

11:40 PM on July 19, 1952, Washington National Airport reported seven objects on their radar – there were no known aircraft operating in that area. The airport's controller tower also confirmed they were on their radar as well. They also observed a "hovering "bright light" in the sky, which departed with incredible speed."[131] At the same time, a pilot waiting to take off also reported seeing six "white, tailless, fast-moving lights" — over a 14-minute period.[132] Andrews Air Force Base (AFB) also confirmed seeing objects on their radar and visually.

Similarly, a week later, on Saturday, July 26, at 8:15 PM, an airline pilot and stewardess on a flight into Washington, D.C., reported seeing lights above their plane. These were soon on the radar scopes of both Washington National and Andrews AFB. A USAF master, Sgt. Observed these, saying, "They traveled faster than any shooting star I have ever seen."[133]

These sightings captured the attention of the press and the public. It also raised concerns with the White House, CIA, and the military. Subsequently, at the request of the President, the USAF was directed to shoot down any UFOs.[134] Over the next couple of years, the previous level of UFO sightings tapered off.

Secret Agreements
President Eisenhower is reported to have met secretly with different ET delegations on two separate occasions, once at Edwards AFB in 1954 and at Holloman AFB in 1955.[135]

The first occurred while President Eisenhower was on vacation in Palm Springs, California. In the evening and the early hours of the following day, February 21, 1954, he was reported as missing. The next morning, he

---

[131] Carlson, Peter; Carlson, Peter (21 July 2002). "50 Years Ago, Unidentified Flying Objects From Way Beyond the Beltway Seized the Capital's Imagination." The Washington Post.
[132] Carlson, Ibid.
[133] Gilgoff, Dan (14 December 2001). "Saucers Full of Secrets." Washington City Paper. Retrieved 23 January 2024.
[134] Michael E. Salla, Ph.D., *Galactic Diplomacy – Getting to Yes with ET,* Kealakekua, Exopolitics Institute, 2013, page 330.
[135] Salla, Ibid, pg. 17.

attended a church service in Los Angeles. In response to the reporter's questions, they were told he experienced a dental emergency and subsequently received treatment. Following this, an independent investigation found this was a cover-up. In actuality, it was determined that he had a *first contact* meeting with ETs at Edwards AFB. Several whistleblowers have since come forward and provided eyewitness accounts of this occurring.[136]

Coincidently, a little over a week later, on March 1, the U.S. detonated the largest-ever hydrogen bomb at Bikini Atoll in the Pacific. This was the only test following the one on November 1, 1952, under the Truman Administration. The timing prompts the question: was this test an answer to ET's attempts to halt nuclear testing?

As it turns out, there are accounts of the ETs creating this period of UFO events to encourage the government to adopt a policy of nuclear disarmament. With the associated concerns to national security – from both within and outside of the Earth – it's understandable why this wasn't adopted.

A year later, on February 10, 1955, President Eisenhower went on vacation, flying from Washington D.C. to Thomasville, Georgia. After arriving, he again disappeared. Only, this time, it was for thirty-six hours. As it turned out, he secretly travelled to Holloman AFB to meet with ETs again.[137] Numerous eyewitness accounts confirm this meeting and observed UFOs present. According to accounts, a treaty with the aliens was agreed upon, with several provisions being reported.

One provision was to keep the ET presence secret, with a mutual non-interference clause. Apparently, this was an agreement made exclusively with the U.S. Most notable was the allowance of the aliens to abduct humans in exchange for technology. The U.S. Government naively accepted the terms of this; thinking these were for medical purposes, and abductees would not be harmed or have any memories. In reality, this resulted in

---

[136] Salla, Ibid, pg.s 48-63.
[137] Salla, Ibid, pg.s 64-70.

abductions for other purposes, including hybridization programs, DNA harvesting, and other even more sinister reasons.[138] As you might expect from a party with the intent to exploit another, the terms agreed upon were interpreted by the aliens as only general guidelines. They were not followed and leveraged by the alien ETs to their advantage.

And, what the U.S. didn't realize at that time is that the agreement *opened the door* to exploitation by these aliens under the provisions of the Galactic Federation – the regulatory body over our region of space. Remember, these exploitive aliens have been doing this for eons. They literally *have it down* with victimizing trusting species such as ourselves. Fortunately, as you'll learn, there are benevolent ETs who have helped us understand this and counter it.

The Internal Division of the U.S. Secret Space Programs
With the signing of the 1955 accord with the alien ETs, the government embarked on a cooperative effort to gain ET technology in exchange for allowing alien abductions and experimentation. This involved MJ-12, the Pentagon (the military), and the CIA. In September 1947, the U.S. Army Air Corps became a separate branch of the military, the U.S. Air Force (USAF). Thus, MJ-12, which is responsible for all matters involving UFOs and ETs, became the controlling agency for this emerging endeavor. The USAF, the Army, the Navy, and the CIA all worked cooperatively – along with select military contractors – to carry out the related activities.

As you've already read, what these agencies didn't realize is that the U.S. Navy had its own intelligence-gathering organization since before WWII. Because of this, when the 1955 agreement was signed, the Navy realized what was really happening. The aliens were the same ones that were allied to Nazi Germany during WWII. Thus, they were continuing partners with the Fourth Reich – the surviving hidden German power. As a result, the Navy not only understood what was occurring with this agreement between the government and the exploitive aliens, but they also had the ability to surreptitiously work around it.

---

[138] Salla, Ibid, pg.71

It's evident that the Naval top leadership took their oath to office to heart – to support the Constitution of the United States and the associated values. This precluded their adoption and integration into the government's work with the alien ETs. As a result, they remained independent, with the outward appearance of being part of the agreement. In reality, though, they took their own path, working with benevolent ETs. This produced the covert space program known as Solar Warden, as mentioned previous chapters. This is described extensively in William Mills Tompkins's book *Selected By Extraterrestrials*. It may read like fiction, but as you'll learn in the next chapter when the government (USAF, Army, and CIA) eventually learned of this (in 2015), it was an enormous shock.

Solar Warden

This is the U.S. Navy's secret space program consisting of a fleet of deep space operations. By the early 1980s, Solar Warden consisted of eight battle groups. This is apparently what inspired both TV series *Star Trek* and *Battlestar Galactica*. As it turns out, Gene Roddenberry had a relationship with Vice Admiral Leslie Stevens' son, who – it is theorized – knew of the Solar Warden  program.[139] This was brought to both the public's and the government's attention by William Mills Tompkins' book *Selected By Extraterrestrials*.

The *twenty-and-back* program referred to by several individuals in Chapter 10, is also revealed by Mr. Tompkins in his book. He stated that this has been employed by the U.S. Navy for Solar Warden since then as well. This is further confirmed by other witnesses.

---

[139] https://exopolitics.org/gene-rodenberry-based-star-trek-on-secret-us-navy-space-fleet/

Summary

If we draw a parallel of the U.S. space technology development with that of aviation technology, it suggests a dramatic progression. At the end of WWII, jet aircraft were introduced. In 1947, Captain Chuck Yeager exceeded the speed of sound (Mach 1) in the X-1A experimental rocket plane.

In 1954, the North American F-100 jet fighter entered service. This was the first USAF operational jet capable of exceeding the speed of sound in level flight.

In 1976, the McDonnell Douglas F-15 entered service with the USAF with a top speed of Mach +2.5. It is still a front-line aircraft to this day, almost fifty years later.

In 1966, the Lockheed SR-71 *Blackbird* entered service as a long-range, high-altitude, Mach 3+ strategic reconnaissance aircraft. Finally, it retired in 1999, and it has not been replaced with any known aircraft.

Realizing the U.S. probably had UFO craft in the 1950s, one can only imagine the level of development today. The quotations (in Chapter 10) by Ben Rich[140], the former head of their Advanced Development Company (commonly known as the Skunkworks division) from 1975 to 1991, clearly suggest the level of technology that might exist today.

At the same time, though, politically speaking, the government's activities have increasingly become more isolated from a Constitutional perspective. Since the late 1940s, the President's and Congress' involvement became markedly less until there was little to no oversight. Fast forward to today, and you can see the latest Congressional investigations into UFOs are

---

[140] https://www.lockheedmartin.com/en-us/news/features/history/rich.html

essentially from the same perspective as the general public – the majority of the members of Congress are no more knowledgeable than you or I. In fact, it's probably less since you are reading this.

Additionally, you'll undoubtedly note I haven't dwelled on the National Aeronautics and Space Administration (NASA). While receiving all the public attention with the nation's efforts in space, the accomplishments pale in comparison to the real covert space programs. NASA was created in an apparent answer to the Soviet space program in the '50s. It was necessary to publicly demonstrate a response – all while maintaining complete secrecy of the ET technology and associated programs.

UNBELIEVABLE

CHAPTER 17 THE TWENTY-FIRST CENTURY

Like the previous period between the end of WWII and the beginning of the twenty-first century, the first two decades of the latter have been full of surprising developments as well. The most notable, and in the public attention, was a total reversal of the U.S. Government's previous complete denial of the existence of Unidentified Flying Objects (UFOs).

A Startling Reversal and Revelation...the 2004 Naval Encounter

As previously mentioned in Chapter 4, the NY Times article reporting on the 2004 Naval encounter with target imagining and involved personnel testimonies clearly marked a dramatic reversal of 80 years of total denial by the government of any existence of UFOs. The photo is from the resulting video taken that day with the UFO. (This video is available from numerous sources by Googling "2004 UFO navy images".)

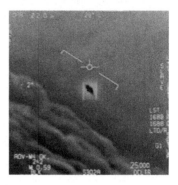

Two Covert Space Programs Reveal

With the publishing of William Mills Tompkins' book *Selected By Extraterrestrials* in 2015, he revealed the U.S. Navy's autonomous Solar Warden space program. This was distinct from, and completely unknown to, the USAF and CIA's covert space program. The former was a cooperative venture with benevolent ETs, while the latter was a collaboration with exploitive ETs. And, while the Navy was fully aware and involved with the USAF/CIA program, they did not share any of their covert program or information with the USAF/CIA.

When the USAF/CIA discovered this reality, one senior USAF SSP officer responded: "They told us we were the tip of the spear, but we found out we're just the f---ing Coast Guard."[141] This reflected the shock of the USAF discovering the U.S. Navy's interstellar Solar Warden space program, in

---

[141] Michael E. Salla, PH.D., *US Air Force Secret Space Program*, Hawaii, Exopolitics Consultants, 2019, page 299.

comparison to their programs' activities being limited to our solar system.

The U.S. Space Force Turning Point
In May 2018, President Trump announced the creation of a sixth branch of the U.S. Armed Forces: the Space Force. This prompted some substantial resistance within the military establishment, as you might expect, with the previous separate programs of the USAF/CIA and the Navy. Despite this, the President signed into law the Space Force Act on December 20, 2019. In addition to combining resources, this resulted in the oversight of these programs being coordinated under the Executive Branch – a dramatic reversal to the establishment of MAJESTIC 12 in 1947 during the Truman Administration. With the involvement of the Nazi Fourth Reich, alien ETs, and the wealthy elite, this is a powerful development; removing their previous influence and control from the USAF/CIA activities in space. The previously hidden support and collaboration with these unseen forces will severely impact their crimes against humanity, including slavery, experimentation, DNA harvesting, hybridization programs, and worse. At the same time, it suggests the return of these activities to oversight within the Constitutional government framework.

A Period of Turmoil
As with the UFO/ET phenomenon in general, much of the activities and knowledge are hidden from the general public. This appears to be particularly true, beginning in 2015 and extending to the present with the politics and related activities with UFOs, ETs, and Earth space programs.

You now know about the revelation coming from an inside whistleblower regarding the separate U.S. space programs of the USAF/CIA and the Navy. This undoubtedly caused great consternation among the different factions of the dark elements of the government and their behind-the-scenes wealthy elite leaders, let alone their alien allies.

Adding to this, and readily apparent, was the transition of political philosophies reflected by the change in leadership in the U.S. and European countries. The result of this was questioning of previous agreements and understandings that were now put in doubt. The principal ones are the NATO alliance and commitments. This resulted in repercussions that are still being felt.

In Chapter 12 on politics, you learned about a little-known but sobering apparent 2018 false-flag event outwardly attempting to create a war against N. Korea. If this actually involved the use of a nuclear weapon, it puts a stark warning out to what unseen elements are willing to do to accomplish their ends. The suspected collaboration between benevolent ETs and the USAF suggests a transition away from the previous CIA influence on this branch of the military, as it's suspected that the CIA commandeered a U.S. Navy nuclear submarine to perform this strike. It certainly could have achieved its desired result, with the inflammatory rhetoric going on between the U.S. and N. Korean leaders at the time. It would have been a new Pearl Harbor, but it would have consequences for all involved of another order of magnitude. Who knows what the repercussions of such a devastating attack would have been?

According to several sources, at the end of the second decade of the twenty-first century (2020), the Galactic Federation decided to address the crimes against humanity by eradicating the exploitive ET's alien presence and influence. This prompted a combined campaign to eliminate the vast underground networks of aliens that have inhabited subterranean Earth for eons, including the Antarctic colonies at the South Pole. According to reports, since then major powers have been in a rush to recover and exploit these resources. In addition, the previous trade with these aliens and their Earth trading partners has been severed. You can imagine the shock to the world leaders when this revenue stream ceased – jeopardizing both their wealth and power base.

It's an interesting coincidence that this coincides with one of the major oligarch nations – Russia – deciding to invade neighboring Ukraine, a source of technological as well as agricultural wealth. This would be a logical development to *fill the gap* created by the loss of their previous alien trading partners, and thus prop-up their oligarchical regime.

Additional activities within the U.S. military hint at internal strife regarding the increasing disclosure of information regarding UFOs and ETs. The acknowledgement of the existence of UFOs by the Navy is one example of this. In Dr. Michael E. Salla's *US Army Insider Missions*, books 1 & 2, he details an experiencer recruited based on his unique abilities. This person's subsequent experiences expose conflict within the military with his access and ability to report what he's learned. It soon becomes obvious that there are different factions involved that do not agree with exposing reality.

As an additional note for anyone wanting more information or detail on what's briefly outlined here, you need only to explore all of Dr. Salla's extensive publications.

PART V THE UNDERLYING ANSWERS

UNBELIEVABLE

CHAPTER 18 PUTTING IT ALL TOGETHER

Inherent Limitations

As an introduction to a *need to know* for the general public regarding Unidentified Flying Objects (UFOs) and Extraterrestrials (ETs), this book is obviously a compromise with conflicting requirements. First, with the overall objective to provide an overview, it is severely limited in what it can present – just based on space available, along with a reader's interest and attention span. Adding to this is tempering the content's believability by only highlighting the major points. There are so many more details that would further test anyone's tolerance for accepting the information's credibility. Yet, many of the details not only add credibility but also emphasize some of the points supporting the overall conclusions being presented. Regardless, the *unbelievability* reinforces the need to identify these limitations on what's being presented. It's an unfortunate inherent constraint on any book of this type.

Reveal No. 1 – The UFO & ET Phenomenon in General

Anyone with any interest in this topic now knows that the U.S. Government has acknowledged that UFOs exist. With this coming to fruition in 2020, it reversed a previous over 70-year policy of denial, cover-up, trivialization, and ridicule of any information or sources regarding this phenomenon. This basically recognizes there are crafts or objects that have been observed that are unknown, often displaying characteristics or behavior that cannot be explained by today's generally accepted science.

It also further suggests and reinforces the suspicion of secrecy with the claim *they didn't exist before*, but *they do now*. We also know of extensive evidence suggesting that humans have been aware of ETs and have interacted with ETs to create UFOs since the inception of WWII. This is with both recovered craft, USN intelligence, and a multitude of other sources. Government UFO and ET activities escalated sharply following the war, with further recoveries of craft and ETs, Operation Highjump, and subsequent exopolitical agreements.

Furthermore, the recent acknowledgement of UFOs exhibiting unexplained technology suggests it is well beyond normal evolutionary developments of scientific discovery like we have witnessed with similar technologies in aircraft, automotive, or even energy in recent history. The resulting obvious question is: if it's not from human sources, where or who is it from? This is the inherent link of UFO technology to suggesting an ET existence. In other words, the source of UFO technology is suggested by both logic and historical evidence.

So, we have several reasons to strongly suspect that Extraterrestrials (ETs) exist – in addition to all the evidence. One reason is the technology associated with the now-verified existence of UFOs. Two, with the coincidental emergence of startling and unprecedented new technologies in electronics and related fields. Ending WWII, electronics utilized vacuum tube technology. In a little over a decade, these were as obsolete as horse-drawn vehicles with silicon chips, printed circuitry, and microprocessors.

Reveal No. 2 – The German ET Alliance and Technologies.
Again, this is revealed by USN intelligence exposing evidence regarding Germany achieving cooperative relations with ETs and their subsequent development of the *Wunderwaffe*, or wonder weapons leading up to and during WWII.[142] Students of this period are familiar with this terminology referring to their advanced jet-powered aircraft, in addition to the V-1 flying bomb and V-2 rocket – both employed against London during the latter stages of the war. Behind the scenes, though, were the real wonder weapons involving the use of ET technology, such as the previously mentioned Haunebu spacecraft employing un-Earthly technology.

As the referenced Wikipedia link below refers to, the former jet and rocket technology is well-known. The ET-based Haunebu, not so much. But, if you explore the latter, you soon realize the evidence is clear that Nazi Germany possessed this previously out-of-this-world technology before WWII.

We also know, based on the same information sources testifying to Nazi Germany's UFO programs, that the U.S. Government became aware of these activities at the beginning of the war, and the resulting secrecy

---

[142] https://en.wikipedia.org/wiki/Wunderwaffe

prevailed over anything associated with this subject. We also know that during and after the war, UFO craft were recovered by the military. This eventually led to post-war efforts to reverse-engineer the technologies associated with these craft. This was coordinated by both military and industry contractors. The resulting developments are well-known, such as fiber optics, printed circuitry, solid-state electronics, microprocessors, and numerous other technologies that emerged during the late '50s and '60s. These developments and their commercialization are yet another striking coincidence with what is generally known.

Reveal No. 3 – Why didn't Hitler employ ET technology during WWII?
Well, there are a number of potential reasons. However, a principal one is fairly obvious, given what you've learned from Chapters 7 and 8. It is a *prime directive* with all ETs seeking to keep their existence unknown to the general population of Earth. For the benevolent and ambivalent ETs, this is to avoid societal disruption (and its associated potential for our destruction). For the aliens with a goal to exploit us and our planet's resources, it provides the most effective means to maximize their profit. And, there's the associated belief common to ET colonizers that it's to our benefit.

Remember, many ET civilizations are thousands – if not millions – of years older than ours. That's the reason their technology is so advanced. But that also means they've gained similar experience with other worlds – specifically exploiting ones such as our own. And what's the most effective method in achieving this? Colonization. As pointed out earlier, they've learned that this is best achieved when the less-developed world is totally unaware of their covert victimization. There's no resistance from the population if they are *in the dark.* And, it's of mutual benefit for all the subversive parties involved to keep this a secret.

Knowing this, we have the alien ETs committed to keeping this secret at literally all costs. Thus, I'd suspect Hitler was prevented from leveraging his ET technology for any tactical or strategic advantage. How would they have done this? It's hard to say, but it may have involved incentives with an offer he couldn't refuse. Or, it might have been coercion combined with potential threats. If one didn't work, the other would.

Given the advanced knowledge and experience of alien ETs, I'd suspect it was through the former, which would have been advantageous in two crucial respects. First, the aliens had a clear opportunity to offer Hitler something he couldn't refuse – the continued survival of the Nazi Fourth Reich. And second, it was an offer beneficial to both, and with that, it continued their partnership and their opportunities to exploit the Earth for mutual profit – a win-win.

The theory that Hitler was given an opportunity he couldn't refuse is supported by remarkable evidence that is typically overlooked. That is, many of the people who have been abducted or gone to facilities on our moon, other planets, and their moons in our solar system; report that German is the spoken language. Accompanying some of this is witnessing the authorities in these locations mirroring Nazi appearances and behavior. Coincidently, it's also reported that President Eisenhower's meeting with one of the alien ETs exhibited a strong German accent. This is a detail that seems inconsequential when encountered, but *taking a step back*, it's quite revealing.

The suggestion here is that Hitler was, in fact, persuaded by his alien partner in their facilitating the continuation of Nazi influence and power. This was with the transfer of German science and wealth to the Fourth Reich based in Antarctica. This, along with the alien partner, provided the dominance of the solar system – militarily, economically (commerce), and politically. If one digs deep enough, this conclusion becomes apparent. While it may be *unbelievable*, history and the considerable evidence supports this hypothesis.

Reveal No. 4 – Subsequent Evidence Confirming this Conjecture
We know that Nazi Germany did not employ any significant ET technologies during the war. This is known history (other than some of the observations of *foo fighters* might suggest). We also know that they possessed this capability, at least to some extent. We also know that in 1946, the U.S. launched Operation Highjump, as described in Chapter 16. Ostensibly, a research mission, in fact, was a military task force aimed at eliminating the Fourth Reich threat that existed in Antarctica. This was unsuccessful due to

the Nazi alliance with their alien partners and the use of advanced ET weaponry that had been transferred during WWII to their South Pole base. Admiral Richard E. Byrd, Jr., USN, the Officer in Charge of this expedition, alluded to this with his subsequent statement to the press when he stopped in Chili – both with the defeat and the consequences to the world with their technology.

However, it doesn't end here. During the next five years, there were increasing efforts by both benevolent and alien ETs to gain agreements. The former was attempting to eliminate the threat of nuclear weapons. The latter were seeking free reign for their rape of Earth's resources – including humans. The continuing escalating encounters of ET UFOs with the military ultimately culminated in public demonstrations aimed at embarrassing the U.S. government of our vulnerability. This basically forced President Eisenhower to meet on two separate occasions (that is known).

For the aliens, this accomplished two goals. First, an agreement met the regulatory requirements of the Galactic Federation, which legally enabled them to exploit the Earth. It's also believed that the U.S. ultimately granted aliens to secretly abduct and conduct experiments on the public in exchange for a transfer of technology to the CIA and USAF. Meanwhile, the Navy was working covertly with a benevolent ET group. Thus, we transition to the USAF and CIA becoming aware of this situation in 2015. Following this, apparently, a faction in the USAF changed loyalties to join the Navy's efforts to protect the public's interests. The CIA apparently continued with the alien collaboration and subversive efforts with their *old wealth* masters.

Reveal No. 5 – Secrecy & Subsequent Exploitation
As a result of all this, we end up with hidden wealthy elite factions that continue to control governments behind the scenes with their enormous wealth and influence. The added collaboration with alien ETs only magnifies this. In the U.S., this was originally greatly facilitated in 1947 by President Truman establishing MAJESTIC 12, a collaboration of the CIA, military, industrial, and scientific leaders assuming complete control of everything related to UFOs and ETs. With this, the knowledge and control subtly shifted from the Constitutional-based government to what President Eisenhower

termed *the military-industrial complex.* His 1960 exit from office speech obliquely referred to this.[143] From here, it only got worse. Subsequent Administrations were greatly frustrated by this escalating shift in power – so much so, it's strongly suggested that it resulted in one of their deaths.

Unbelievability No. 6 – More Recent History
With all this, we end up where we are today. The initial reports in 2004 of confirmed sightings of UFOs by the USN. These resulted in the formal acknowledgement of their existence in 2017. This was followed in 2018 by a suspected attempt at an apparent nuclear holocaust, where Hawaii was attacked by still unknown agents (CIA at the direction of factions of the wealthy elite?). Apparently, a collaboration of benevolent ETs and our military thwarted this.

Even more recently, there have been reports of benevolent ETs basically becoming fed up with alien exploits and eradicating their physical presence on the Earth, along with their associated influence. It's clear that this would have impacted their illicit trade that has literally surreptitiously raped mankind for decades. The recent added international unrest and division points further to an unseen source for this. And, the timing is certainly coincidental with the war in Ukraine.

Unbelievable No. 7 – Where We Are Today
Even more recently, continuing reports suggest that the U.S. military's – shift away from the wealthy elite, CIA, remaining corrupt government agencies, and the alien influence – is gaining strength. This is with reports of efforts to further expose the reality of ETs with even more revelations and evidence. Added to this is the increasing number of ET artifacts being uncovered in relation to developments. However, at the same time, this reveals continued conflict with those trying to maintain secrecy.[144]

Where this will end up remains to be seen. The next chapter delves into this in more depth. With the previous knowledge, the possibilities of potential outcomes are narrowed. Yet another *need to know.*

---

[143] https://en.wikipedia.org/wiki/Eisenhower%27s_farewell_address
[144] Michael E. Salla, *Insider Mission books I & II,*
https://www.amazon.com/s?k=insider+missions+book

UNBELIEVABLE

CHAPTER 19 THE REAL REASONS FOR THE SECRECY

Introduction

When one begins to realize the associated secrecy with Unidentified Flying Objects (UFOs) and Extraterrestrials (ETs), a few reasons for it become relatively obvious upfront. One is the military advantage it could provide. With the advanced technology, it's apparent that any country possessing this would have an enormous advantage over those that don't. Thus, secrecy offers a clear advantage and immediate solution to these concerns.

And, of course, there are also the related societal concerns involving religious, cultural, and fears – coming from our learning we are not alone, we may not be a superior species, and the realization that we apparently live in a relatively underdeveloped world. And finally, given our Earth's history, we know what typically happens to less-advanced cultures when confronted with a superior society.

However, as you may have realized from reading this so far, there are a multitude of other hidden concerns that are raised with the UFO and ET phenomenon that involve substantial additional political, economic, and human factors. Combined, these create the earlier-mentioned Pandora's Box dilemma, which presents both opportunities and threats to our society. The following specific concerns include the many identified and underlying reasons for sustained secrecy. And, like most issues, your opinion on these will likely depend on your perspective and beliefs.

Overview

Remember, at this point, the government is the active agent managing secrecy, with various hidden wealthy elites exerting influence through their political funding and physical powers. For those performing the associated functions within the government, there are substantial deterrents to exposing these covert activities. Prosecution, loss of benefits, and even loss of life are potential consequences. Thus, only a few brave whistleblowers come forth, either not bound by confidentiality agreements, close to death in their later years of life, or ones that defy the threats. Some have paid with their lives. And, while recent laws have been enacted to address this, behind the scenes fear undoubtedly still remains.

The secrecy imposed by the government is claimed to be the ultimate level of silence, even surpassing that involving the development of nuclear weapons during WWII. The following are the reasons why. I'll start with the most obvious.

1. Mega Opportunity & Threat

If you are a world leader, you see UFO/ET technology as both an opportunity and a threat. Both hinge on total secrecy. The opportunity is to employ ET technology and related exopolitics[145] (relations with ETs) to your advantage – politically, militarily, and economically – to optimize influence, power, security, and profit. Similarly, the threat comes from all of Earth's other competing entities seeking this same advantage. If you were to allow them to achieve this end, it would be at your loss. Thus, the goal is to gain and maintain this obvious advantage. To ensure this, secrecy is simply an integral component to achieving this success.

2. Advanced Technology – A Pandora's Box

In itself, and regardless of who possesses it, ET technology similarly poses both threats and opportunities to society as a whole. For a world experiencing climate change coming from burning fossil fuels, the prospect of enabling other renewable and non-polluting energy sources is enticing. Some theorize that we are surrounded by virtually infinite energy. If this is true, it may be possible to tap into this source and essentially eliminate the pollution associated with our current primary energy source. Imagine the benefits to society with this and the other related aspects of this type of technology. One can only speculate on the new products and services that might become available for all of us to enjoy. Your imagination may be the only limit with this future at this point, with so little known of what any advanced technology might offer.

But there's also a hidden dark side to new technology. It introduces change, uncertainty, and disruption – with some pre-existing industrial segments being substantially threatened or, in many cases, completely replaced.

---

[145] https://exopolitics.org/

There are countless examples of past products suffering this fate, including slide rules, typewriters, film photography, audio and video cassettes, CDs, and vinyl record manufacturers. Some still exist and even have had a resurgence of popularity, but nothing compared to their prime. In these cases, the trauma experienced in peoples' lives remained mostly out of sight to the general population, but with ET technology, it would affect everyone.

With energy, the change involved would be on an entirely new level. Virtually every element of our society is based on fossil fuels. We're not talking about one industry or even a segment of the economy. To gain additional insight into what this might entail, the recent introduction of electric vehicles (EVs) into the automotive marketplace better illustrates this.

With EVs, the automotive industry is currently in a quandary – not knowing the direction of the regulatory requirements, customer preferences, or future core complementary technologies like battery developments. Replacing internal combustion engines (ICEs) with motors sounds simple, but it literally redefines the entire vehicle in many fundamental respects. The associated redesign, supply chain, and planning requirements with their lead times impose substantial risks and threats to existing manufacturers. This doesn't address any of the associated supporting segments of the automotive industry, such as parts, maintenance, tools, training, and associated providers. And don't forget brick-and-mortar supporting industries such as electric/gas utilities, fossil fuel suppliers, and their supporting infrastructure.

I'm using the transition to EVs to provide a glimpse at the immense complexity and potential impact of transitioning to ET-based advanced technology. The transition to EVs currently is directly impacting only a small portion of the transportation industry. ET technology would impact every sector of the economy with redefined energy sources, equipment manufacturers, and every other aspect involved. Current fossil fuel providers might virtually go away, with the subsequent devastating shock to our global economy.

While it's clearly beneficial in the long run, the threats from a sudden transition would want to be avoided or at least deferred. You can see how this is similar to the previous opportunities and threats; it produces winners and losers. If you are a world leader, global business owner, or anyone else concerned with your economic well-being – you are *risk averse*. In this case, with the oil industry dominating virtually every aspect of the economy (and probably politics), you can begin to appreciate the influence being exerted behind the scenes to avoid or delay this transition. This leads directly to the next reason for the secrecy.

3. Fossil Fuel Subsequent Lost Future

The loss of wealth, profitability, influence, power, and prestige to all leaders associated with the oil industry is a major deterrent to releasing ET technology. To put it simply, wealth is power. The fossil fuel segment of the economy dominates the world which is dependent upon its energy sources. These powerbrokers – which include the wealthy elite mega-corporation owners, as well as all world leaders such as oligarchs of oil-rich nations, elected officials, and their subordinates – are all where they are because of the wealth generated by this segment of the economy. Continued denial of society's access to ET technology is the only path to the continued success of the fossil fuel segment of the economy and their power base.

4. Exposing the Real Source of Power

While everyone knows the current price of gasoline, few realize the extent of the oil industry's hidden influence and power. If ET technology were to become public, the previous roles of the current covert powerbrokers would be exposed through recent history. This would result in their censure and ruin, in addition to any future significant leadership roles. Again, secrecy is key to this being avoided.

5. Secret Government Agreements

Exposing past government agreements – such as that by the U.S. Government in the mid-fifties – is yet another threat to the government and associated leaders in industry, science, and religion. Allowing exploitation and kidnapping of citizens in exchange for technology would not be viewed favorably. This would seriously jeopardize the continued viability of our government as it exists today.

6. Subsequent Prosecution & Censure of Involved Parties

From the 1940s to the present, elements of the wealthy elite, dark components of the government, and associate contractors have conspired to commit crimes. Some politicians have violated their oaths of office by circumventing fundamental provisions of the U.S. Constitution. Others, including members of government agencies and the military, have been guilty of violating both national and international laws – including crimes against humanity.

An inevitable outcome of ET disclosure would be to ultimately reveal the history of the last 100 years or so and the associated ingrained corruption of the U.S. government. This would result in public outrage, prosecution, incarceration, and associated social and political unrest, along with the associated political and economic turmoil. For anyone in these positions, this only adds to the previous concerns. Thus, continued secrecy in hiding the truth is imperative. It's a survival issue for many.

7. Exposing Our Vulnerabilities

Politically speaking, it's useful to remember that the primary responsibility of any government is to ensure its own survival. The previously mentioned concerns with national security are an integral element of this goal. The existence of ETs relates to the last thing any government wants to reveal – its vulnerability and, thus, implied failure of those responsible. This is an added factor for political leaders to continue the secrecy concealing any existence of ETs.

8. Maintaining Stability & the Status Quo

Another fundamental aspect of the government's role, in addition to national security, is to ensure the continued health and well-being of society. The overall economy drives much of this. Thus, Wall Street and the government are dedicated to avoiding disruption and ensuring stability. This is directly threatened by the UFO/ET phenomenon as well as the associated technology. Both detest change, and there's nothing – short of war or a major disaster – that would present a more formidable challenge to any nation. So, there are convincing arguments by both experts and patriots to continue the secrecy. For them, it's less about *what's right*, than *what's best* for the overall nation as a whole.

9. Climate Change & Conflict are Profitable

Another consideration is some industries also benefit from the current status quo. Climate change is one example, as it provides opportunities for businesses in building construction and materials. Wars are also extremely profitable for those producing weapons. In the case of the latter, it's in the best interest of the military to ensure their future. An added consideration with continued secrecy.

An economy focused on short-term profit and stock market performance places little value on any long-term benefits. This, and placing no value on environmental issues, creates a situation where many people are motivated by the present, having little or no concern for the long-term future since they won't be around, and there's no immediate profit for them to change.

10. Added Political & Defense Industry Opportunities

Continued secrecy about UFOs and ETs provides an opportunity to manipulate the public's knowledge, specifically to create a false threat that would boost defense spending as well as strengthen the government's powers. This would create economic benefits, serve as a rallying point, and be a distraction from issues that would normally be of a public focus. Artificial threats are witnessed today by some authoritarian governments for these purposes.

11. False History

Imagine how society would react to learn that a faction of Nazi Germany in the form of the Fourth Reich survived. And, through the integration of their former intelligence service officers and scientists, they were able to thrive after WWII becoming embedded into our government – totally unbeknownst to the public. That, as a result of their continuing collaboration with ET exploitive aliens, they were able to coerce the U.S. into allowing citizens to be subject to abductions, abuse, slavery, and even worse? The shock of this type of revelation would undermine anyone's faith in government, let alone our society as well. Secrecy is the only way to avoid this reality.

12. False Comfort – Avoiding Inconvenient Truths & Realities
Many people have difficulty with current events as they are known. Imagine the stress, disruption, and losses coming from exposing the reality of ETs and associated issues – including conflict – in the Universe. This would further erode any semblance of status quo or stability for much of our society. Another reason for secrecy.

13. Loss of Faith with Existing Institutions
Science and religions would similarly be impacted by the discovery that ETs are real. The inherent weaknesses of our scientific institutions and experts would be revealed with the funding of projects depending on the support of the government – with its sinister motives in this case. Many religions would take a similar *hit* with their common beliefs and histories. Neither the scientific or religious communities would want to face this truth.

14. Jeopardizing How Governments Work Today
The reality of UFOs, ETs, and our governments' actions should provide a clue as to how secrecy is integral to their current functionality. It greatly simplifies decision-making in democracies, as well as even autocracies. The less people know, the simpler the issues are, with similar benefits to decision-making in general.

15. ET Needs for Secrecy
As mentioned in Chapter 8 *Why Don't They Reveal Themselves?*, ETs are fully *on board* with the need for complete secrecy regarding their existence. The benevolent and those indifferent realize the potentially disastrous impact their presence might have on human society. However, the real influence comes from the alien ETs that want to exploit Earth. Their experience shows that the inhabitants are totally unaware of their victimization, which offers the optimum form of colonization. As a result, they fully support the continued secrecy of their existence as well.

16. The Hidden Alien Influence
The suspected surreptitious political influence furthering the alien agenda is yet another reason for secrecy. This influence would explain how the

moral, ethical, and ability to reason have been seriously jeopardized in recent decades. It appears to align with both the wealthy elite and alien's agenda to transition to a form of government more easily manipulated and favorable to enhancing their profits and power.

Summary

Thus, aside from the obvious national security and related surface societal disruption issues, one soon learns of the myriad hidden deeper concerns. Particularly among those who make high-level decisions involving secrecy. For these powerbrokers and their agents, in both government and business, their very survival depends upon secrecy. For these players, no other factors are significant.

What's right is inconsequential with all but the most principled patriots in the military, or ones of similar character in business and government. With the most credible whistleblowers who have come forward, these are typical traits evidenced by their testimony.

For the in-the-know elite without these attributes, the choice is simple and clear. What works for them, is what's best for society in general. To gain an appreciation for this conundrum, the following chapter briefly reviews the stakeholders and their objectives involved with this topic.

PART VI PERSPECTIVES

CHAPTER 20 STAKEHOLDERS AND THEIR OBJECTIVES

With the critical keystone role of secrecy, it's useful at this point to briefly review the stakeholders involved, their motives, and resulting objectives. The previous chapter covered many of these, summarizing the many reasons behind the secrecy involved with Unidentified Flying Objects (UFOs) and Extraterrestrials (ETs).

The Secrecy Decisionmakers
As you'd expect, most of those that command the secrecy have the most at risk. These are in two distinct groups. One is the high-level government leaders involved in dark activities and the hidden wealthy elite influencers behind the scenes. Of course, the other is the exploitive alien ETs.

As outlined in the previous chapter, the first depends upon secrecy to ensure their very survival. For those founded in the oil industry, their power base depends upon it. For these and others, their activities relating to ETs have put them at risk of criminal prosecution, humiliation, and censure. Secrecy is the only policy ensuring that they continue their life as they know it.

But, beyond survival, many of these leaders realize the potential opportunities with ETs. And, to ensure these, secrecy is yet another crucial requirement – to keep their competition in the dark.

The Involved Subordinate Leaders
These are those that are responsible for the management and control of the secrecy. Similar to the high-level decision-makers, they are also *at risk*. Their incomes, reputations, and careers literally hinge on continued secrecy. If their masters fail, they fail. Those most at risk also face criminal prosecution for complicity in the crime's governments have committed.

The Front-Line Participants
This group would include military, government, and related personnel (such as contractors, researchers, and other scientists) who are following orders and doing their jobs. Recent changes in U.S. laws now are aimed at protecting them *if they come forward* as whistleblowers. Within the

limitations of this, though, there are still significant deterrents for most individuals to do so. Impacts on their careers, respect from their peers and leadership, and the usual threats, including physical harm and death. While the law may theoretically offer protection; the reality is that often, there's a high price to be paid.

The Unknowing Majority

I'm assuming this would describe you. Otherwise, you probably wouldn't be reading this. Without a basic understanding of the topic of UFOs, ETs, and everything involved, *you don't know what you don't know.* This is the reason why everyone has a fundamental *need to know.*

Without some semblance of this knowledge, you are *at risk* – in more ways than anyone would imagine. And, if you are part of a democratic political environment, you are unable to participate effectively. Combined, these create a dangerous situation where unknown entities may be trying to victimize or enslave you at best, and even consume you at worst.

And, as extreme as this may sound, it's a potential reality. The aliens that allied themselves with Hitler and the Third Reich were not acting in the best interest of the planet or the human race. When they repelled the U.S. task force in 1947 in the Antarctic, they were not merely defending their realm. This is evidenced by their subsequent coercion in the 1950s to force an agreement to terms allowing the aliens full access to interfere with Earth. The subsequent extensive abductions, kidnapping, experimentation, enslavement, and worse are further evidence supporting this real threat to humanity. Obviously, this is *a need to know* in any society.

The Real Hidden Stakeholder

This covert plot is orchestrated by the ultimate entity in control and with the most to gain. These are the alien ETs with the goal of exploiting Earth's resources – minerals and biological. As pointed out previously, this is most effectively accomplished through an unknown colonization of the planet. And, if you think about it further, it's most effectively accomplished through autocratic rulers, whether they're based on wealth, as in oligarchies, or based on reverse racism, such as in monarchies. This is why so many democracies are facing unprecedented challenges today.

Simpler autocratic governments are much easier to control and manage. Recent trends in Western politics reflect hidden influences trying to accomplish these ends. Obviously, this is debatable and is clearly described as a conspiracy theory, but there are strong similarities evidenced by some current leaders and their followers in this direction. These characteristics are strikingly similar to those seen in Germany during the founding of the Third Reich where alien influence was involved.

There's evidence to suspect these ET aliens employ hidden technologies aimed at influencing susceptible humans. There's actually an author who has written a series of books on this threat. They're titled *The Allies of Humanity* by Marshall Vian Summers.[146] In these, he points out that ETs prefer to resolve conflicts through influence. Armed conflict is avoided – as a last resort – due to its destructive waste of resources. If only the human race would achieve this insight!

The Bottom Line
Each of these stakeholders has different perspectives, motivations, and objectives. While it may seem they also have differing levels of risk, I'd argue the opposite. It's clear which has the most power, and secrecy is the only protection to their continued success. But, I'd suggest that everyone has a stake in this matter – that we all are exposed to extreme risk of one sort or another.

Those with the most power face certain losses with disclosure. At the other end of the spectrum, those who are basically unaware of any of this also face the risk of failure in the form of victimization, enslavement, or worse. Unfortunately, we don't know enough to determine the probability of any of the outcomes with disclosure of the reality of ETs.

One thing is certain. Each player has different perspectives, motivations, and objectives. On one end, the alien ETs and the powerbrokers quite likely think it's in the best interest of the human race to be exploited. In this way, the benefits will outweigh the costs to the majority. It's a similar belief

---

[146] https://www.amazon.com/Allies-Humanity-Book-Marshall-Summers

expressed recently by a U.S. State governor that slavery benefitted all.[147] Unbelievable, but unfortunately true.

The Question of Disclosure

This returns us to evaluating the policy of secrecy based on *what is right* or *what's best*. The answer depends upon the individual. If you're selfish, the answer is clear for those imposing the secrecy. If you are of a more selfless incline, you may still face a conundrum. One can certainly argue *what's right*, but the question of *what's best* remains. Exploring this further begins with the topic of disclosure, the subject of the following section.

---

[147] https://www.nbcnews.com/news/us-news/new-florida-standards-teach-black-people-benefited-slavery-taught-usef-rcna95418

PART VII DISCLOSURE

UNBELIEVABLE

CHAPTER 21 DISCLOSURE – THE PROCESS

Disclosure Definition
The Merriam-Webster dictionary provides the following definition of the term *disclosure*.[148]

> *Disclosure* – 1) the act or an instance of disclosing: exposure
>
> 2) something disclosed: revelation

Introduction & Overview
The term *disclosure* in reference to Unidentified Flying Objects (UFOs) and Extraterrestrials (ETs) denotes the removal of all secrecy around this phenomenon. It is exposing the truth.

On the surface and without further thought, disclosure – revealing the presence and reality of UFOs and ETs – appears straightforward and simple. Once you've read this chapter, though, you'll have a new appreciation for the hidden aspects of this topic. First, you'll realize that it isn't a singular event, but a process. And, what you'd think would be clear and well-defined is emerging as a similarly complex conundrum – much like the other aspects of the UFO/ET phenomenon.

One of these is the realization that the process has begun, prompting a multitude of other questions. These include: *How, Why, Why now*, etc.? And, like the entire topic, they don't have clear-cut, known reasons. We are left with hints and subsequent conjecture as their answers.

The Process Has Begun
This bears repeating; with the U.S. Government's acknowledgement of the existence of UFOs, we have achieved the first step in the process of disclosure. UFOs are real. It's official. A seventy-plus-year strict policy of denial has been partially lifted with the entire UFO/ET subject.

Partially is a keyword here. Obviously, with the existence of UFOs now

---

[148] Meriam-Webster Dictionary, https://www.merriam-webster.com/dictionary/disclosure

being officially recognized, this is a dramatic turnabout from the previous secrecy of the government. This is probably why the numerous questions associated with this haven't yet entered the discussion. Some of the most obvious of these issues are as follows.

Why now? What has changed? What implications does this have with prior reports regarding UFOs? It would seem to suggest that some of the previous accounts would now be validated. It's arguably implausible that all the previous sightings and encounters would be bogus, while recent incidents are valid. If so, how would this be explained? These questions lead directly to the following.

In other words, does this acknowledgement of UFOs being real reflect a change in policy? Or is it the result of previously new, unseen phenomena? This might seem to be an esoteric question on the surface, but it strikes at the core of the shift in policy. It's not an academic question. It has real consequences for the subsequent discussion.

An obvious question related to UFOs being real is, who are they? Where do they come from? This crucial question hasn't yet become the focus that you'd expect. Not that it's impossible, but the capabilities evidenced by the U.S. military UFO sightings clearly demonstrate technology that is well beyond any generally known science today. It represents a leap in knowledge that challenges any suggestion of it being an evolutionary development in human progress. As a result, an immediate question comes to the forefront: is it ET technology?

Following this, for close observers of government policy, there's been a notable shift regarding the question of ETs. In years past, the government treated the issue of ET existence identically to the issue of UFOs. They did not exist. Total denial. Now it seems – associated with the acknowledgement of UFOs – that they *may* exist, but there's no evidence they do. It's notable shift in policy that the potential existence of ETs is now no longer specifically denied. The official position continues to refute there is any evidence of ETs. As with the previous, the question relating to this subtle shift in policy also does not appear to have received any attention.

Aside from all these questions, disclosure began with the official U.S. government declaration that UFOs are real. The secrecy regarding this one element of the UFO/ET phenomenon has partially been lifted. This is most significant, but at the same time, it just prompts more questions. And, as more are addressed and uncovered, the process of disclosure comes to include the internal political and exopolitical aspects as well. You can surmise why the process continues to be impeded with the first step in acknowledging the existence of UFOs.

The Disclosure Process
With the previous discussion, you now realize that disclosure can involve a progression of reveals rather than a one-time exposé. With the disclosure of the reality of UFOs, we're experiencing what appears to be this form of release of information. For this reason, it's useful to review how this process might be described. This now has more relevance since it appears to be occurring. Another important point is that this is only a guide outlining what a full disclosure process might entail.

An actual process could vary substantially from this, either by only consisting of portions or by altering the order of the elements. It would be configured to meet the needs of those in control (assuming that it is a *controlled* release). At the same time, it's important to realize that it's not only those who seek secrecy who are in this position. Disclosure could result from it being forced upon them by other stakeholders involved.

It's also worthwhile to note that once this process begins, it will be increasingly difficult to stop it. Exposing any of the realities just leads to additional focus, credibility, and questions, further jeopardizing the secrecy of the entire subject matter and related components. If you examine the questions identified previously regarding the acknowledgement of UFOs, this quickly becomes evident.

Following any revelation of this impact, it appears there's a period of *shock*, followed by a focus on the details (the *trees*). It apparently takes time for – all but the experts – to realize the importance of the related overall underlying questions that are subsequently raised (the *forest*). It's like trying to *put the genie back in the bottle*. The continued attempt by the government to direct the focus on details is further evidence of this.

STAGE 1

This represents the first step in disclosing information pertaining to the UFO, ET, and related phenomena. With the U.S. Government's disclosure of the existence of observed UFOs, we are experiencing this initial phase of the disclosure process. This is the acknowledgement of the existence of one of the major components of the UFO/ET phenomenon. There are many remaining questions about UFOs, but their reality has been confirmed – thus making the topic of UFOs credible. A major first step is disclosure.

STAGE 2

The obvious next step concerns the second principal component of the UFO/ET phenomenon, addressing the reality of ETs. In reviewing Chapter 19 *The Reasons For The Secrecy*, you quickly realize the consequences of what this next step entails. It's one thing to recognize there are unexplained observations. It's an entirely different level to accept that we are only one of many ET species in the Universe. Associated with this is also the reality that we're technologically behind – with all the potential concerns.

Connected to this are all the various ways ET's existence could be revealed. It could be done factually, with full information about all the known species, their intentions, and involvement. Or, it could be done as a *false-flag* threat or event (attack). This clearly depends upon the intent of the parties involved in initiating this stage. It would also determine if any of the following stages would occur, let alone what order they may be in. It's simply difficult to predict this, not knowing what, if, why, or how these phases would encompass or occur.

STAGE 3 and Those Following

Depending upon the intentions (or accidental release)

resulting in Stage 2, here is where a number of different scenarios may play out. Taking a positive approach (to minimize the societal concerns with disclosure), several would likely focus on the future. One could announce the discovery of a benevolent ET species. Another option would be to reveal the reality of countless ETs and the associated exopolitics involved – both within and outside our solar system.

Another form of disclosure could reveal the past, with the hidden history of alien interference, specifically with Nazi Germany, WWII, and subsequent events. It's unlikely this would be a planned release of information due to the obvious repercussions to government, industry, the economy, and society. This would expose all of the crimes and concerns that have occurred. It's obvious the existing powerbrokers will do everything in their means to avoid this. This leads to the next potential direction.

The least favorable scenario would be a *false-flag* scenario. This could occur in several ways. One would be by announcing an alien species with evil intent. More likely, though, would be to *stage* an alien attack against the Earth. This is a very real prospect because first, it may be a *last resort* for the wealthy elite/corrupt government leaders to survive, and second, the ET technology that is now available to some governments and their militaries can facilitate this. Experts now generally acknowledge that many – if not most – UFO sightings now are the result of Earth-origin UFOs, not ETs.

With a *false-flag* scheme, no further factual information would be exposed. At least not by the perpetrators. It's possible that others *in the know* could try to mitigate this direction. But, at best, that likelihood is questionable and of doubtful success. Even if the sources were credible, it's open to debate whether society as a whole would be receptive or responsive to their efforts. In all likelihood this information would be accepted as is UFO/ET knowledge is now.

Summary

At this point, it's useful to realize that the U.S. Government has begun a process of disclosure. In doing so, this has essentially cracked open the UFO/ET *Pandora's Box*. How this unfolds and to what extent remains to be seen. Similarly, few people seem to realize the significance of this going forward. It's not just about UFOs, but the remaining pieces of the puzzle. We now know there is actually a UFO piece to the puzzle. This is a positive development in many respects, but it's a foreboding one in others. This is the focus of the following chapters.

UNBELIEVABLE

CHAPTER 22 REVELATIONS

This chapter temporarily takes *a step back* from the progression of developing the topic of Unidentified Flying Objects (UFOs) and Extraterrestrials (ETs) contained in this book. This is an interim review of the insights provided. It's important to do this at this point for two reasons. First, it is particularly relevant to this and the following chapters. Second, it's quite likely that many – if not most – readers will have discounted much of this text's content due to disbelief. As a result, some of the substance and its importance may not be fully realized or recalled. Thus, a brief review is useful at this point.

The Secrecy
Regardless of the believability of the previous content, it should provide at least a somewhat different perspective on the entire topic of UFOs and ETs. At this point, I'm hoping you've gained at least a deeper appreciation of what this subject matter entails. It's not just about the details of UFOs, ETs, and their technology. It also involves a history of government denial, cover-up, deception, trivialization, and ridicule. This reveals a concerted effort to keep anything relating to this topic concealed from the public. Reports consistently state this subject matter is of the highest level of secrecy in the U.S. and, at this point, you have at least an appreciation of why this exists.

Subsequent Questions
Obviously, the immediate questions are specifically about UFOs and ETs. But, as the real reasons behind the secrecy suggest, there's a lot more involved. In addition to the technology questions, there are societal concerns, as well as those of hidden elements of critical importance to our nation.

The recent acknowledgement of the U.S. Government confirming the existence of UFOs has, as this book suggests, unveiled entirely new dimensions to the pre-existing conundrum with this topic. It's only the beginning, as new – and now – more credible questions arise and become an increasing focus of the general public. This is evidenced by the U.S. Congress taking a renewed interest in this direction. This will place even more emphasis on what is occurring, as well as what's happened in our recent past – both within and eventually including WWII. This is also evidenced by recent testimony highlighting Operation Paperclip, which will lead to other revelations occurring since then.

What is being witnessed is the initial phase, triggering an eventual acceleration of increasing interest and questions. All resulting in increasing knowledge and awareness of the UFO/ET phenomenon and its scope.

Revealing Recent History
Operation Paperclip may very well lead to revealing the Nazi ET-based technology. Maybe not, but there's plenty of other evidence that would. This is similar to Operation Highjump and the subsequent rash of UFO sightings in the 1950s. Then, with the evidence of President Eisenhower's meetings with ETs on two separate occasions, the pieces of the puzzle begin to come together.

The evidence is admittedly scant on the surface, but a *deeper dive* reveals multitudes of independent, credible sources confirming these suspicions. Germany, with an alliance with an alien ET species, acquired UFOs. While there was no known use of this technology during WWII, its transfer to Antarctica was also similarly documented. It soon becomes apparent that an innocuous-appearing scientific expedition to the South Pole was, in fact, a military task force aimed at eradicating the German/ET alliance. With the evidence pointing to a defeat, the subsequent years of escalating UFO encounters in the U.S. further suggest a concerted campaign by ET factions to coerce the government to formally sign agreements with the parties involved.

One benevolent ETs seeking to eliminate nuclear weapons was unsuccessful. Another, with the surviving Fourth Reich remnant of Nazi Germany and their alien ally, was successful. With this, it's apparent that the U.S. agreed to formally allow alien access to human experimentation and exploitation. This was in exchange for them sharing ET technology.

It turns out the U.S. didn't have a chance in fighting the latter outcome. With Operation Paperclip, both former Nazi scientists and intelligence agents became embedded into both U.S. advanced technology and the highest levels of the government. They knew what we had, and what we were planning.

Countering this was the USN's independent intelligence during and after the war. This, and their subsequent development of technology and space programs, were totally unknown to the remaining infiltrated military and government (USAF/CIA). When this was uncovered in 2015, many in the USAF realized they were *on the wrong side*. An incident confirming this was the later collaborative effort downing a nuclear missile aimed at Hawaii. This involved the USAF, USN, and benevolent ETs.

These elements of the U.S. military have demonstrated their allegiance to their oaths of office in support of the Constitutional protections provided to citizens. Unfortunately, this same event confirmed that the CIA continues to be a tool of the hidden elite/dark government secretly continuing to collaborate with exploitive aliens. And, even while more recent efforts by benevolent ETs have made substantial efforts to eradicate the aliens, their human partners continue to exert their wealth and political-based powers. The invasion by Russia coincides with this and suggests an effort by their oligarchs to replace their previous alien trade and profits with the opportunities in Ukraine.

An Important Point
Your perspective and openness to consideration of conspiracy theories, combined with the extent of your knowledge of all this, determine its believability. It's obvious that *on a good day*, some – if not all – is based on conjecture. But, it's also obvious that there is a wealth of clear facts supporting all this. First, the pieces of the puzzle fit, and second, they explain what's been observed in recent history. Third, the evidence supports the conclusions. Finally, it confirms what would otherwise be credible proof of what is being presented.

Of course, none of this makes it *believable*. That's OK. It's both something to think about and, more importantly, information that expands your awareness of the scope of possibilities involved with the otherwise seemingly solely academic nature of the UFO/ET phenomenon. It may not seem real, but what if it is? It still is *a need to know.*

UNBELIEVABLE

CHAPTER 23 THE CONSEQUENCES

This brings us back to where we left off with disclosure and all the different scenarios that could be involved. It's not all about questions about UFOs or ETs, but it encompasses so much more, as you've learned, regardless of whether you believe it or not.

From this point on, the focus is on *what's next*. It's important to understand the significance of achieving the first stage of disclosure, which is recognizing that UFOs are real. Taking a step further, the underlying realization is that this has cracked open the UFO/ET *Pandora's Box*. It's irreversible. A path has been taken, and while there are a lot of different directions from here, there's no way back.

With the UFO component of the overall phenomenon becoming viable, it prompts the credibility of all the pre-existing questions, along with new ones, about UFOs and relating to them, ultimately leading to the inevitable next stage: Do ETs Exist?

Which of these is going to be more difficult to answer? Is this Earth-based technology? Or is it of ET origin? Either answer serves to further open the *Pandora's Box* model. Both imply a massive cover-up. The first might be explained by national security concerns and resulting measures. But, it also leads to difficult questions that have, at best, embarrassing answers with the funding, cover-up, denial, etc.

But, more importantly, with either answer, the technology is revealed as being real. And, if you review the reasons for secrecy, you face the same concerns with the overall impact on society, the powerbrokers, and their alien masters. So, little has been avoided. You may have removed much of the criminal conspiracies, but the threat to the economy and everything related to the oil industry is still one step closer. This is bad news for much of the wealthy elite since this is a dominant portion of old wealth. Of course, this is also true of the related benefits of the new technology energy – which can't be overlooked.

Thus, we face a conundrum similar to the one previously revealed by the acknowledged existence of UFOs. Only now, the process of further disclosure is set in motion. It's already increased the public's (and conventional government's) attention. It's made the UFO/ET topic viable, with the admission of the UFO component being real. With these combined, added questions are going to come to the forefront, with it being much more difficult to avoid their subsequent answers.

The end result of all this is: What Comes Next? To attempt to answer this, we have to return to recent history.

Conjecture as to Why UFOs Became Real
What we know at this point is three events contributed to the government's acknowledgement of UFOs. First, UFOs made themselves present to USN personnel. In the past, this would have been subject to the continuing secrecy policies. For some reason, this didn't occur. Whether it was intentional, by mistake, or a combination of those two is yet unknown. Second, USN personnel were free to reveal their observations of UFOs. This included openly discussing them with the media, as well as the USN sharing targeting imagery involved with the encounters. This was unprecedented, and it supports USN leadership's involvement in the decision-making. This leads directly to the realization that there are elements in the military, the government, or both that have the fortitude and desire for information on this topic to be released. Something has changed. This never happened in the past.

Now, why this shift occurred is still a matter of conjecture. But, if we review recent history, it offers some possible insight. We know that, prior to 2015, only the Navy branch of the military was aware of the real truth involving alien exploitation. Shortly after this, the USAF not only became aware but some of its leadership appears to have shifted its alliance to opposing continued collaboration with the involved exploitive aliens. With the apparent growing support within the military and associated increasing awareness in the government, it appears that it has emboldened the involved leadership to act. Whether the intentions are noble or otherwise, the direction is clear. UFOs are real. Denial is mute at this point. The first step in the disclosure process has begun.

There's actually further evidence supporting this. In Dr. Michael E. Salla's two recent books, both titled *U.S. Army Insider Missions*[149] , he provides insights coming from an individual recruited by the USAF as a result of UFO/ET experiences combined with his unique abilities. What's pertinent to this, is he's confronted with several incidents of being both included in ongoing UFO/ET military activities, and excluded at the same time. It's readily apparent that there are conflicting groups within the military (or above) that are directing his involvement.[150]

This suggests confirmation that there are two opposing views on whether UFO/ET information should be revealed to the general public. There's actually nothing new with this. It's reported that this was a question posed in the original MAJESTIC 12 oversight body established by President Truman in 1947.

James Vincent Forrestal (February 15, 1892 – May 22, 1949) was the last Cabinet-level United States Secretary of the Navy and the first United States Secretary of Defense.[151] As such, he was the initial appointee of this committee. He is also believed to have been a strong advocate for sharing knowledge about UFOs and ETs at that time. What is known, is he subsequently died after being admitted to the National Naval Medical Center, having jumped to his death from the sixteenth floor of the hospital. Whether this was a suicide or another way of resolving this issue remains a mystery. But, it has remarkable parallels to similar events involving this topic in U.S. history.

In short, there is evidence that those wanting the public to know the real truth about UFOs/ETs have gained enough strength to influence the previous long-standing policy of outright secrecy. It's difficult, with what's been revealed here, to underestimate the importance of this apparent radical shift.

---

[149] https://www.amazon.com/US-Army-Insider-Missions
[150] https://www.amazon.com/US-Army-Insider-Missions-Underground/dp/0998603899
[151] https://en.wikipedia.org/wiki/James_Forrestal

Direction

Where this leads is clear at this point. First, for all the reasons described, this direction is further jeopardizing the remaining efforts at maintaining secrecy. Regardless of the question of ETs' existence, the technology is undeniable. And, as you've learned, technology is the key to many of the resulting opportunities and threats to society. It would appear, regardless of what direction follows, that the technology is going to have to be faced eventually.

As the previous chapters suggest, the powerbrokers and others in favor of concealing all this appear to be increasingly *backed into a corner*. Obviously, they are going to try to mitigate this as best they can. But, equally apparent is that this is also going to become more difficult – both as their opponents continue their efforts and as time goes on with the increased interest, added credibility, and new questions continuing to arise.

CHAPTER 24 OPTIONS

From the previous chapters, understanding the motivations of various stakeholder groups provides insights into what has occurred in recent years. It also suggests what options might exist, and particularly, their potential likelihood.

Secrecy Failure Modes – Options
Since this issue involves full secrecy, it's all about keeping information from the general public. This is important to remember because there are a number of failure modes associated with this strategy. One, is someone *in the know* who releases information. This actually has occurred numerous times with both known and anonymous whistleblowers.

Consistently, these have been subject to denial, cover-up, deception, trivialization, and ridicule, as previously described. As a result, a lot of this information remains out of the public eye. However, the recent release of unquestionable evidence ending the secrecy of the existence of UFOs redefines the results of this occurring in the future. With the Navy's validation, the presence of UFOs is now undeniable.

Secrecy is also jeopardized by a party introducing evidence of the existence of ETs or the exopolitics that have been involved over the last 100 years. There is a wealth of this having occurred. And, while much is credible and normally would be considered evidence, it's still subject to the same denial and lack of interest witnessed by anything often related to UFOs and ETs.

The third option would be for either a rogue ET or other group to force acceptance *on the public* of their existence. The first is probably unlikely since there's been no apparent effort to do this before. Arguably, there may be incidents where their presence has been evidenced, but the same denial and lack of interest, for the most part, has always seem to have prevailed.

The option of an ET species or group coercing the dark powerbrokers to release the knowledge of their presence is also probably unlikely. But it's apparent that this situation may be changing. First, with the benevolent collaboration with the U.S. – and presumably other militaries – and second, with recent activities reported. One is the eradication of the alien presence and trade with Earth. Another comes from other activities that are occurring in Dr. Salla's recent books. In these two volumes of *U.S. Army Insider Missions*, there's a clear collaboration with international governments on activities that will result in an ET existence becoming obvious. Thus, the day may be approaching when this could occur.

Actually, another consideration is that this is what prompted the U.S. Government to acknowledge the existence of UFOs. Probably unlikely, but not without precedence (the rash of mass flyovers in the 1950s), or in the realm of possibility.

And, the final option is the previously mentioned *false-flag* scenario.

Considerations
For those wanting to maintain secrecy, best mitigate the consequences, and possibly manipulate disclosure to their advantage, a *false-flag* event has a number of obvious advantages. First, it can be initiated and managed by the *bad actors* to achieve the desired results. Second, it offers the potential to avoid revealing ET technology and all its consequences – by claiming it is unavailable from the ETs involved. Similarly, they have the opportunity to minimize the risk of exposure and prosecution of their crimes and collaboration with aliens. Furthermore, the obvious shock and fear that could be created would distract from all other concerns. This would serve to defer, or with associated political changes, avoid any further revelations or the truth being revealed. Another contributing factor would be the allied aliens coming out as potential winners from this as well – either as *rescuers* or just remaining out of sight as they are now. It's a potential *win-win* for the *bad actors* and any aliens involved.

From the perspective of the old, wealthy elite, their military supporters, and corrupt government officials; this is a *win-win* scenario all around. They're potentially *back in the saddle* and would possibly be able to re-open the previous trade channels with alien entities. It could ultimately lead to a very similar situation to what is presented in the previously mentioned movie Captive State, only that the public has no knowledge of the colonization of Earth.

Another scenario could unfold where the two opposing factions (involving the secrecy) were to negotiate a compromise. This potentially could mitigate some of the benefits and threats. This would be accomplished by agreeing as to the *what, how*, and *when* the information is released. A lesser evil than a *false-flag* scenario, but one with substantial concerns remaining. It's likely these concerns would prevent both parties from agreeing unless there was a benevolent ET influence coercing both parties to cooperate. And, as unlikely as this may appear, it is a possibility – given the reports of a benevolent ET group eliminating the presence of aliens and their trade with Earth. This may be the most realistic and favorable scenario to hope for.

I've left the following option last, principally because it is probably the least likely. This would be where the champions of secrecy acquiesce to full disclosure. It's simply never going to happen. Too much is at risk. The loss of everything they value, combined with the devastation it would cause. This is essentially a *suicide* option for them. It's the reason for all the secrecy in the past.

Summary
So, in conclusion, we're left with two different directions, both with numerous potential variations. But, like much of this subject matter, it's less about the detail than the overall direction. I think it's apparent from the previous information that the *false-flag* option has a lot of appeal to those who've had complete control over secrecy in the past. As this control has apparently waned, this entails more inherent risk of being exposed. Thus, they may have to face the inevitable – acknowledging the existence of ETs. As I said, it would appear that they're increasingly being *backed into a corner*. In situations like this, a *survival mode* surfaces. This, and the obvious advantages, would suggest that this direction is a very real possibility.

On the other hand, the potential of a benevolent ET influence can't be ruled out – particularly with the growing behind-the-scenes support and collaboration with the military and sympathetic government leaders.

CHAPTER 25 CHOICES

This chapter is the final instance of an *unbelievable* fact. This is about disclosure or revealing the truth about Unidentified Flying Objects (UFOs) and Extraterrestrials (ETs). For all those who believe *total disclosure* is *what's right* and necessary (like I did until recently) you're going to face another reality that you might want – and be tempted to – deny. But, as you well know, wanting to or being tempted by something doesn't necessarily produce favorable outcomes. And, this is a case where *what's right* may not be *what's best*, but in fact represents *what's worst*.

The Threat
This provides another example where Extraterrestrials (ETs) have shared insights that we need to learn. Undoubtedly, experience has shown them the necessity for their existence to remain unknown for less advanced societies such as ours. I'm not referring to exploitive aliens here, but including the benevolent and observer ETs that, at best, want to help us but, in any case, don't want to harm us.

In one of the books I read while doing my research, there was a reference to one instance where an ET species revealed itself to a society comparable to ours, and it resulted in their annihilation. At the time, I didn't really recognize the full significance of this. But, at this point, considering the subject of disclosure fully, it becomes apparent they had learned this from experience firsthand. And, further consideration leads to a potential real validity of this knowledge coming from their experience.

This is Not Conjecture – Political Considerations
Think about political experiences that have occurred in recent history. First, there were cases where crimes and corruption were suspected by U.S. presidents. First was the resignation of President Nixon in 1974. This caused a crisis in the government. It was unprecedented and resulted in considerable uncertainty and disruption. A similar case more recently involved the President being impeached on two separate occasions. Even without his leaving office – and probably because of it – it offers a similar example of disruption, unrest, and uncertainty. And, everyone knows the continuing saga of this with the subsequent claims and multitude of

pending legal cases.

Without dwelling on either of these, consider the magnitude of concerns with *all* the high-level officials in each of the three branches of government. The executive branch could include the president, vice president, and all the cabinet officers. It would certainly include many of the members associated with the CIA and military, let alone all the national security agencies involved. In Congress, numerous members would have to be involved as well, with those on *insider* committees. In the Supreme Court, this might be the only branch that would remain untouched by the complicity, but think of their subsequent involvement in the litigation.

With any unveiling of the scale of this crime, corruption, and treason, imagine the disillusionment of the public at large. Any doubts about the viability of our current form of government? And, associated with this, putting the government *back on its feet*. The process of accomplishing this, along with measures to prevent this from ever happening again, is mind-boggling.

An incident involving a political catastrophe of this magnitude raises a very real concern that our system of government, as it exists now, would not survive.

Technological Considerations
Chapter 19, *The Real Reasons for the Secrecy*, provided a brief introduction to the concerns about introducing radically advanced technology into our society and the economic disruption that would result. A radical transformation in the energy sector would produce repercussions throughout virtually all others in our economy. Like the political unrest and trauma, a similar experience would result in the economy and, thus, in everyone's lives throughout the world.

Added Economic Concerns
With the two previous considerations – political and technological – the economic wealth would be undermined. The stock exchanges would plummet to incomprehensible new lows, eliminating many peoples' investments, along with associated wealth. This would only contribute to

the calamity that would follow.

Societal Concerns
In fact, reviewing Chapter 19 also suggests all the societal issues that would arise if full disclosure were to occur. Reiterating these include 1) a total upheaval in maintaining political and economic stability; 2) exposing our vulnerability of our society – with all the related concerns, trauma, and anxieties – with the realization of the existence of ETs and that we're not at the top of the *food chain*; 3) the associated impact on those of faith, with their comparable concerns and questions; 4) discovering much of the history of WWII is inaccurate at best; and 5) all the added uncertainty, anxiety, and risks from learning the added complexity of a new reality.

Putting This in Perspective
First, let's review some recent events that have disrupted our society. In the U.S., 911 in 2001 traumatized the Nation with the terrorist attacks that resulted in approximately 3,000 deaths. In the 2008 Recession, American households lost an estimated $16 trillion in net worth; one-quarter of households lost at least 75 percent of their net worth.[152] In 2020, the outbreak of COVID-19 resulted in 1.5% of the U.S. population dying, with the dramatic impact on the world's economies from the resulting supply-chain issues and associated shortages, etc.

One of the most significant recent concerns – and completely overlooked – relates to the cover-up of the 2018 incident involving what appears to be a *false-flag* attack on Hawaii. It's easy to disclaim this as real, but the facts speak otherwise. First, the subsequent claim that it was a *mistake* by the local authorities conducting a drill. The military facilities in the vicinity were responding to the threat accordingly, and they did not utilize state agencies for this type of threat. Second, a warning was issued. Third, many observed an object exploding in the atmosphere at the time. Fourth, this was reported in the local media but soon was covered up. Fifth, related activity by numerous Coast Guard vessels occurred in the area of the observed explosion. Six local witnesses and the community were warned to remain silent on what they saw. Finally, subsequent information has added to the

---

[152] https://www.britannica.com/money/great-recession

credibility of this occurrence, explaining why it happened and how it was avoided. In short, it did happen.

Given this occurred, imagine its significance. First, who would initiate this? Who is capable of this type of attack? Why would they do it? Most importantly, what would be the potential consequences of this?

To gain an insight into the latter, the population of Hawaii in 2018 was 1.4 million. If the attack involved a nuclear warhead, it's safe to say that any previous experience – short of what occurred in Japan at the end of WWII – would even approach the order of magnitude of the loss of life and devastation this would have caused.

Was this a *false-flag* staged attack, deviously designed to achieve the desired results without any reference to UFOs/ETs?

Now, given the previous incidents referenced in recent history, you can guess the trauma this would have caused. At the time, the toxic rhetoric involving the U.S. President and the leader of N. Korea had reached an all-time high. For many people, it would be clear where this attack originated from – even though that would be completely false. Remember Pearl Harbor and what that precipitated. It's entirely logical that whoever initiated this obvious *false-flag* strike had a similar intent.

However, one of the key points with putting this in perspective and considering the possibility of this *false-flag* event is that it's already occurred. So, that removes much of the doubt that this could ever occur. Whether it makes a similar subsequent event more or less likely is difficult to tell.

Conclusion – A Need to Know
I'm summing this book up with *be careful of what you wish for.* Thinking the U.S. government should acknowledge the existence of ETs and provide insights into the remaining questions and knowledge (as outlined by this brief review of exopolitics and history) involved would have catastrophic consequences.

First, acknowledging the existence of UFOs has laid bare the previous cover-up of UFOs over the last 80 years since the '40s. Second, this suggests a similar secrecy and previous falsehoods of denying the existence of ETs. Third, this is further supported by a strong likelihood of ETs as the source of the technology observed with acknowledged UFOs. Given these, it further reveals covert government policies to conceal not only the technology and knowledge, but also the inherent deception and extortions involved. This is further supported by the chain of events and related evidence with recent histories. There's a clear trail of events leading to the conclusions presented in this book. It's only a matter of time for this process to play out.

As stated in the beginning, the goal isn't for you to believe what's presented but to consider it. The first step in the process of disclosure has begun. There's no denying that. This should provide some clues as to what might follow. This should be of great concern and a *need to know* for anyone. Most people are interested in this topic; they want to know and believe there should be a full disclosure of everything associated with it. I hope you understand now: 1) why that's not likely to occur and 2) the risks associated with it.

In 2017, a turning point occurred when UFOs were acknowledged, and the U.S. initiated the disclosure process. This was the first step to sharing information that could result in the end of the world as we know it. How this process is subsequently managed will determine our future. Given the parties involved in this decision-making – with their contrasting values, motivations, and intents – do not instill confidence in a favorable outcome. One positive consideration is that we have ET friends who undoubtedly have faced this before. Hopefully, they may play a key role in getting us past this conundrum.

What's notable is, the unbelievable nature of this text's content doesn't detract from this conclusion regarding disclosure. *What is right*, isn't necessarily *what is best.*

UNBELIEVABLE

APPENDIX

The following references were contributing resources of the content in this text. These are included only to facilitate further study for those interested. This is only a small portion of the information available on this topic.

1. ***A Gift From The Stars*** *– Extraterrestrial Contacts and Guide of Alien Races* by Elena Danaan
2. ***Alien Contact*** *– Top-Secret UFO Files Revealed* by Timothy Good
3. ***Alien Interview*** *–* by Lawrence R. Spencer
4. ***Alien World Order*** *– The Reptilian Plan to Divide and Conquer the Human Race* by Len Kasten
5. ***American Cosmic*** *– UFOs, Religion, Technology* by D.W. Pasulka
6. ***Ancient Alien Ancestors*** *– Advanced Technologies that Terraformed our World* by Will Hart
7. ***ANONYMOUS*** *– CIA Agent Reveals the Truth about UFOs* by C. Ronald Garner
8. ***Antarctica's Hidden History*** *– Corporate Foundations of Secret Space Programs* by Michael E. Salla, Ph.D.
9. ***Area 51*** *– An Uncensored History of America's Top Secret Military Base* by Annie Jacobsen
10. ***Area 51*** *– Conversations with insider Stephen Chua* by Elena Danaan
11. ***Area 51*** *– The Revealing Truth of UFOs, Secret Aircraft, Cover-ups & Conspiracies* by Nick Redfern
12. ***Beyond Area 51*** *– The mysteries of the planet's most forbidden, top secret destinations* by Mack Maloney
13. ***Beyond Esoteric*** *– Escaping Prison Planet* by Brad Olsen
14. ***Black Swan Ghosts*** by Simeon Hein, PhD
15. ***Bringers of the Dawn*** *– Teachings from the Pleiadians* by Barbara Marciniak
16. ***CASEBOOK*** *– on the Men In Black* by Jim Keith
17. ***Ceres Colony Cavalier*** *– An account of a twenty-year abduction* by Tony Rodrigues
18. ***Close Encounters of the Fourth Kind*** *– A Reporter's Notebook* by C.D.B. Bryan

ABOUT THE AUTHOR

Having worked in numerous positions with several diverse firms, as a Registered State Professional Engineer with both MBA and BS Engineering degrees, Tim retired after a 30-year career with a local energy utility.

In this latter role, he was part of a team that led to unanticipated and unprecedented success – going from literally struggling to survive, to thriving, along with numerous other accomplishments.

To share the insights coming from this success, he authored numerous trade publication articles, and a book outlining best practices for these groups to redefine their success.

Since then, a unique set of circumstances re-awakened a childhood interest in UFOs and ETs. This led to over 5-years of study, reading over 180 books and related sources of information. The end result of this, revealed startling new answers and a *need to know* for everyone.

Made in the USA
Las Vegas, NV
18 August 2024